The Flayed Man

SOFT SKULL
NEW YORK

The Flayed Man

Chloe Lauter

The Flayed Man

This is a work of fiction. All the characters, organizations, and events portrayed in this novel are either products of the author's imagination or used fictitiously.

First Soft Skull edition: 2026

Library of Congress Cataloging-in-Publication Data
Names: Lauter, Chloe author
Title: The flayed man : a novel / Chloe Lauter.
Description: First Soft Skull edition. | New York : Soft Skull, 2026.
Identifiers: LCCN 2025052857 | ISBN 9781593768256 trade paperback | ISBN 9781593768263 ebook
Subjects: LCGFT: Horror fiction | Monster fiction | Novels | Fiction
Classification: LCC PS3612.A93259 F53 2026
LC record available at https://lccn.loc.gov/2025052857

Cover design by Victoria Maxfield
Cover images: landscape © Wirestock / iStock,
woman © Leandro Crespi / Stocksy,
yawning cat © Atakan-Erkut Uzun / Stocksy
Book design by Laura Berry

Soft Skull Press
New York, NY
www.softskull.com

Printed in the United States of America

10 9 8 7 6 5 4 3 2 1

For my love

I am lonely, I am lonely
I am lonely, I am lonely

—S, "Vampires"

The Flayed Man

1

MIDNIGHT IN THE EMERGENCY DEPARTMENT BRINGS the squeal of old tires and reckless laughter. An antiseptic gasp like an agonal breath, and the big glass panes of the automatic doors grind down the sand in their tracks, revealing the gift left behind by a pickup full of teenagers: one of their own, nineteen at best, swaddled in a stained gray hoodie. He breathes out through a mouthful of broken teeth, and the stains multiply. He smells like malt liquor and tobacco-swilled backwash and the dust-and-dog-shit mélange of the concrete he busted his face on. He smells like blood.

I'm hungry.

Chaney mumbles something and slips out of the other swivel chair as the kid shuffles up to the desk, looking like I'm about to give him detention. He makes a noise like all the fight's gone out of him. It's because he's alone, I know it without having to ask him. His friends ditched him and he's scared, and he's supposed to know what to do. And he doesn't.

"I think I broke my nose," he slurs. Fat, shiny red drops hit the desktop. His blood stinks of reheated food from cans and boxes and flat Diet Coke choked down on a legally mandated thirty-minute break, of furious bursts of iron and desperation as his heart demands he answer for his crime of living.

I'm tempted to sweep a finger through the pooling droplets and pop it into my mouth—I don't know the last time I actually *tasted* blood—but I can't do that here. Someone's always looking.

I slide him a clipboard. Bruising has already stained the bridge of his nose, beginning to stretch beneath his eyes. The muddiness of his words owes less to the liquor and more to the blood trickling down his throat.

Somewhere above my head and a little to the right, Chaney coughs. Black coffee scalds my nostrils. Buys me a second to clear my head.

"You okay?" Chaney drums at her steaming paper cup with perfect almond-shaped nails. "You look like you could use some coffee too."

Chaney smells like vanilla body wash and does her own French manicures and wears pastel-pink scrubs like some kind of triage ballerina. She'll move on from the night shift in a couple months, like everyone does, and she'll meet someone nice and have a couple of kids, and when the white wine comes out, she'll describe the horrors of the ED to her in-laws. I won't figure in those stories. She'll remember my face, maybe, but she'll have forgotten my name. She'll wonder, briefly and without interest, where I ended up. And the answer will be nowhere. I'll still be here, cycling through the same endless nights and pitiful days filled with a different, worse kind of suffering.

Anyway, Chaney's all right.

"I'm good," I tell her. "Bathroom break."

Some days I relish pushing the boundaries of my hunger. Breathing deep when a bloody patient rolls by, holding off feeding till my veins rattle. Proves that I'm in control: of my appetite, and of other things too. Like disappointment. Like anger. But some days, like today, I leave it a bit too long. Enough to remind me that it's not a game. I head for the hall and swallow a couple of times to get my saliva flowing, sniff a few more to clear the clinging afterglow of the kid's blood from my nose. Just make it to the break room. To the lunchbox in the back of my locker, to the Vacutainer vial inside, waiting for me to—

"Karsten!" My name pulls me up short just as the PA crackles to life. *Dr. Avagyan to the emergency department. Dr. Avagyan to the emergency department.*

Avagyan means a trauma case. The nurse who shouted for me closes in, a blur of maroon scrubs and squealing sneakers. "Lady flipped her car with her kid in the back," she pants. "ETA four minutes."

"E32 and 33 are open, I'll—"

"Chaney's on rooms, I need you to log the EMS report." She shoves a clipboard into my chest. "Here's everything they called in. We need patient names to get them in the system."

I could get to the break room in four minutes, maybe. But probably not back again, and the medics rarely stick around long.

I find a corner and gulp down half a cup of black coffee so hot I feel it in my nasal passages. Then the ambulance screams up and the doors gasp open, and I smell blood and asphalt and plastic and dirt and blood and blood and blood.

Mom comes in first, bag valve clutching her face like a

parasite. A gold hoop dangles from one ear. The other ear, the whole other side of her, is cracked cartilage and bone ground down where it shouldn't be. Nurses descend and the salt-and-pepper medic hands her off and she's down the hall. I swill more coffee over my aching gums.

Then the kid. I see the gravel-torn soles of her tiny sneakers first. The kind that light up when you stomp. One's flashing red, faintly. The second medic, stocky and snub-nosed with a shaved head, has her arms braced on either side of the girl's skull, immobilizing her spine, and she's curled over the girl, whispering something to her. I've seen this pair before, rolling in with a woman stuck full of epinephrine and screaming about how she'd sue the cheap casino buffet that let the lobster touch her rice, and before that, with a happy-go-lucky college student drugged at a party, head lolling as her friend wobbled after her in ankle-turning heels. Rodriguez is the older one. Rodriguez, and . . .

"Zawadski," Rodriguez snaps. The nurses have closed in on the girl, but the younger medic—Zawadski—isn't giving her up. Her shoulders heave, and she folds up tighter.

Rodriguez repeats her name. The PA blares. Someone is shouting about the handoff. The empty cup crumples in my hand, waxy and alien. Not food, never was food.

"Vera," Rodriguez says, quieter than everything else happening around us, and Zawadski's head snaps up. Nurses flow into the cracks. The girl disappears. Zawadski stares after her with brown eyes so big you could curl up and sleep in them.

"Get a coffee," Rodriguez says, just as quietly.

Zawadski scowls. At him, at me. "I'm fine."

"Get a coffee."

She stalks past me, the sleeve of her medic jacket glancing

off my shoulder, and under the chemicals and adrenaline I catch the faint scent of particle board and a scabbing cut. When I turn back to Rodriguez, his expression tiptoes between vigilance and accusation. It stays that way as he runs me through the patients' names and all the details they didn't have time to call in, scene description and treatment responses, and I scratch it all down on my clipboard.

There's a tightness in my gut. Not hunger. A seeping secondhand shame. Witnessing Zawadski do something wrong, and worse, sticking around while she was reprimanded for it. I'm not sure I haven't done something wrong too, just by being there.

The break room's empty, the laminate tabletop littered with half-drunk Diet Coke cans and Starbucks cups. No one stops me in the hall. I flip the lock of the bathroom and breathe in the bleach-burnt blank slate scent of tile and air. The anemic hospital lights paint a pink film over the sink and toilet and fold-up changing table. The weave of my jawbone hums as I wash my hands and check my veins, as I unpack the lunchbox and peel back the plastic backing on the disposable syringe, as I pull the blood into the barrel and make a fist of my left hand. The blood smells like solvents and floor cleaner, and I'm so hungry I don't fucking care. When it hits my veins, my knees fail beneath me, and as I collapse into a heap of flesh and want and will, the curse locked inside my chest lifts its head, a howl rising behind its teeth.

Thirty seconds later, I'm in control again. I spit into the sink and swear I'll quit testing my limits. I'll be better from now on. I'll be the daughter my mom deserves.

I want the break room to be empty when I return, but instead I find the pair of medics huddled around the table.

Rodriguez is muttering something too quiet to hear, his hand on Zawadski's shoulder. Less comforting her, more anchoring her in place. She sniffs long and deep like she's trying not to cry, and right then they both realize I'm there.

Rodriguez looks worn out, all the carnage he's witnessed peeking through the places where his skin's too thin. Zawadski just looks angry. She chews her lip and glares at me with big, brown, shiny, furious eyes, and the blood-soaked animal inside me snaps to attention. She looks like she's daring me to get my teeth around her and bite down.

I could. Suddenly, I want to.

"Can I help you?" Zawadski snaps, and I remember what's real and what's not. What's real is that these two are pissed at each other, and at me, and at least one of them is just pissed at the world in general. I'd better get back to work before the night gets any messier.

"Sorry." My tongue's too big in my mouth. Will she sense it? "Sorry. I'm leaving."

They pick up muttering again as I dump my lunchbox and retreat, doing my best to pretend I'm invisible. I brush past Zawadski, feel her flinch away, and the last thing I smell is the salty tang of a scabbing cut, of a semi-healed wound picked open enough times to scar.

2

THE KID WITH THE BROKEN TEETH IS STILL THERE, bloody face to the ceiling and one thumb working furiously over his phone screen, when I head for the dawn outside the ED's sliding glass doors. The TV screens blast true crime reruns on mute. Close-up photo of a woman's smiling face. Wide shot of the house she was killed in. Five in the morning smells like boredom, like bad breath and disinfectant and the sweet rancid odor of packed-in, half-asleep bodies still waiting, always waiting, as the sky shifts with agonizing slowness from black to gray to blue. Busy night. It's always a busy night, somehow.

My car is littered with hair ties and drive-through napkins and a scrunched-up sweater, periwinkle except for a slash of brownish gray down the front where I spilled coffee and chased it with bleach. Dust sticking to the air vents and an empty to-go cup on its side in the passenger seat. My mom didn't raise me to be this messy. Then again, I've disappointed her in much bigger ways.

Twist the key, and the engine sputters. I try it again. Faster, then slower, then fast again, like maybe I can trick it into starting if I move quick enough. It doesn't work, of course. It's just an engine.

I press my forehead into the cracked leather of the steering wheel and picture the jumper cables shoved in the back of the pantry. All I want is to run my errands and go home, to wash the night out of my hair and sleep before the Las Vegas sun gets so bright it blinds me awake for hours. A sudden urge to cry grips me by the throat.

I should text her. Maybe I shouldn't, maybe she's sleeping. It'll only worry her. Unless she's awake, unless she's alone and confused and her only lifeline is the Post-it I left on the door that said, *I'll be back by six. Love, Ellis.*

Why is this so hard?

Hey Mom, it's Ellis. No, she doesn't like that. She knows who I am. I delete it, start again. *Hi Mom. I'll be home a little late, my car didn't start but it's nothing to worry about. I'll call Uncle Bill for a new battery. Joanne's number is on the fridge if you need anything. Don't worry please. Love you.*

She calls almost the same moment as I send it. Like she's been staring at her phone, waiting.

"Hi, Mom."

"Where are you?" She sounds worried.

"I'm at work."

"Don't lie. It's five in the morning."

"I work nights. Remember?"

She sighs, and even over the phone I can read her tone well enough to understand each breath's secret meaning. "Yeah, baby, I know. I'm not a two-year-old, you don't have to talk down to me."

"Sorry."

She pauses, and I hear her slippers shuffling over the kitchen linoleum. "When are you coming home?"

"Did you read my text? I have to stop by Uncle Bill's on the way home for a battery and, you know." Blood, for both of us.

More shuffling. Maybe she's rereading the Post-it on the door. Or maybe the one on the fridge—*Ask Ellis before you take something out of the freezer!*—or the stove—*Turn off the burner when you're done!*—or the kitchen table—*Grocery list is next to the sink!* The fridge door clicks open and shut disconsolately.

"Are you at the fridge?" Could be hunger's making her fussy. A vial of blood, injected intravenously, is usually enough for a full twenty-four hours, but she's needed to feed more often lately. Like as she fades, hunger is filling in the gaps.

"Yeah."

"Get a snack and turn on the TV, okay? The remote's on the table, you can watch something you like. *Night Court*?"

A long silence punctuated by the click of the fridge door. Open, shut. Open, shut. "You'll really be home soon?"

"Yeah, Mom. Of course."

She sighs again. "Are you sure? You know what happens when you lie, baby."

The *baby* jabs like a sharp fingernail. Where other kids have Bloody Mary, people like us have flayed men. They call them by different names, tell different variations of the story, but the gist of it is the same: a creature like us who turned on his family. Devoured their hearts, and in return was cursed with eternal life. Or blessed, I guess. Depends on the telling.

My mom's flayed man story, passed down from her mom, was of a monster who stalks firefly-lit swamps, fangs machete-sharp, unable to return to his human form. I don't know whether he can read minds in the original version, or if my mom added that part herself. When I was in elementary school, if she thought I was keeping a secret, she'd stand in the bathroom with all the lights off and pretend to talk to him until I begged her to come out, swearing I'd never do anything wrong again. He was her way of warning me: if you lie to your mom, if you choose anyone over your family, there are consequences.

"I'm sure." I can't deal with this right now. "I promise, everything's fine."

Another long silence. The smack of a door, more shuffling. Then, finally, slightly muffled, "Ellis?"

"Yeah?"

"Where are you? It's five in the morning. Are you in trouble?"

I peel my fingers off the wheel one by one and count the things I know to be true. It's my job to take care of her. It's not her fault that she gets confused. She's only worried because she loves me. "I'm fine, Mom. I'll see you soon."

I hang up before she can ask any more questions. The sky outside is the same indifferent gray as the concrete of the parking structure. This time, when the engine coughs and refuses to turn over, I feel like screaming.

The tap on my window makes me flinch.

"Hey." Zawadski fills the entire window with the thick-padded navy blue of her medic jacket. "Need a jump?"

I do need a jump, and if it were anyone else asking, I'd be drowning in gratitude. But seeing her resurfaces the prickly strangeness from earlier, and something else too. A sudden instability, like this is the last step of a complex dance I didn't know I was doing. Or the surreal silence before an ambush.

"Sure." I climb out of the driver's seat. "Yeah."

Her car's almost as old as mine, and with at least ten times as many dents. She strips off her jacket to dive under the hood with the jumper cables, red in one hand, black in the other. One bicep is a mess of bruises in various stages of healing. A circle of rich purple mottled with red dots, fading to brown, then green, then yellow bleeding into her elbow, making oil-slick shimmers where it crawls across round, shiny craters of scarring. A nicotine patch is plastered across the back of her other arm.

She jerks her chin up. "Back in the car."

As I pass her, I smell old wounds again, clotted and scabbing, and the soft smooth wetness of regeneration beneath. Zawadski idles her car for a couple minutes, and when I turn the key, my car starts like there was never any problem. What if there wasn't? What if I imagined it or just forgot how to start a car? What if the thing ravaging my mom's brain is in me too?

A smack on the driver's side door pulls me back. Right. This is what's real. The rumbling car and Zawadski's expression halfway between embarrassment and sympathy as she mutters, "Give it another minute, okay?"

When we lean against the car together, side by side as the metal shudders under us, I discover her hair isn't shaved, just slicked flat to her head with gel that makes it look more black than brown and smells like artificial lemon. She's shorter than I expected, with lips that tilt up at the corners and shoulders that slope in like she's using them to form a barrier between herself and the world.

She folds her arms over her chest. "I'm sorry for being a dick to you earlier."

The car hums expectantly. I'm not sure what she wants me to say.

"It's just, you know. Kid stuff gets to me sometimes." She's staring intently at the concrete seam at the corner of the parking lot. "That girl we brought in, she's eight. Second grade. She was already having a tough time at home, and now a hospital stay . . ."

"It's okay," I assure her automatically. "Certain stuff gets me too."

I picture the teenager's bright blood spattering my desk. Such a waste.

"I've seen you around." Zawadski turns on me with eyes that seem to want to pin me in place and dissect me. "How long have you been on nights?"

"A while."

"You like it?"

I work nights because no one stays on the night shift long, no one bothers me much, and because during the day, I need to be there for my mom. How will she be when I get home? Confused and concerned, or furious at some perceived betrayal? Or the worst one, the unnatural docility, like something sucked her essence out and left nothing but numb flesh. My mom loves me more than she loves anything, or anyone. All she wants in return is that I love her too, that I keep nothing from her, that I let nothing take me away from her. Why is that so hard for me to do?

"Yeah," I say, because it's a lot easier to answer Zawadski's question than my own. "It's peaceful."

She scrunches her nose, revealing crooked canines. "Yeah, if your definition of *peaceful* is getting screamed at while you're trying to save someone's life."

I laugh a little, partly because she has a point and partly because I don't know how to explain what I mean. At the hospital, I'm only a bit player in someone's worst day. I'm not the cause of it, and I don't have to be the solution. The people who whine and argue with me over the paperwork or the wait time won't even remember my face by the time they leave.

Zawadski reaches to scratch the middle of her back, and her tank top rides up to reveal a big white bandage stuck over her hip, the same side as the massive bruise on her arm. Then she sticks out her hand with decisive ferocity and says, "I'm Veer. By the way."

Her hand is warm and a bit clammy. My knuckles come away with a light coating of dirt and engine oil from her fingers. "Ellis."

"Cool." She nods to herself. Then, again, her focus is on me, as intense as high beams on a night road. "You're probably fine to get home now. Let me give you my number."

My stomach twists, and I try to remember what's real, and what isn't.

"Just in case you need another jump," she finishes.

We exchange numbers. She gathers the jumper cables and slings her jacket over one shoulder. I slide into my still-running car and watch her in the rearview mirror, a sliver of hair slipped free to curl over her temple, tongue tracing her upper lip as she drives away. My curse growls softly, a curious tremor in my chest, and for a second, I don't mind being an animal. I might even like it.

3

"I HAVE A GUY," UNCLE BILL SAYS WHEN I CALL HIM from the road, asking if he can help me change my battery.

Uncle Bill always has a guy. It's better not to ask too many questions.

"Corolla, right?" I can hear him writing it down. "2014?"

"2012."

"That's fine. I'll help you put it in when you get here."

"How much do I owe you?"

"Don't worry about it. We're family." An acerbic undertone of *can't believe I have to do this* creeps into that last statement.

I ignore it, like usual. "Thanks, man."

My stomach growls. The curse in my heart needs only blood, but the body around it needs more. My mom and I used to laugh at the TV monsters with their cartoonish capes, the way they recoiled in the sun, the way they slept in dirt and never died. Maybe it was like that for some people, once, but not for us. We heal fast, sure, but we're not indestructible. And we only avoid garlic because the smell's off-putting, same as any other pungent food. Sometimes our eyes come out funny in photos if we're not quick enough to duck out of the way of the flash, but our bodies are mostly just like everyone else's, and they can only take so much living.

Uncle Bill clears his throat. "How've you been?"

I answer the question he really meant to ask. "She's okay. About the same."

"Still with it enough to be a royal pain in the ass."

"She doesn't mean to be. She can't help it."

There's another pause, and I think he's waiting for me to say something more, but I'm too tired to have anything much to say. Uncle Bill was a teenager when my mom was in kindergarten, and she hadn't seen him in almost three decades when she showed up in his driveway with nowhere to go and me in the back seat. "Be nice to your uncle," she reminded me constantly in the sixteen years since. Especially when he covered my nursing school tuition, and when one of his work buddies helped get me a job at the hospital. Given all that, you'd think we'd have a better relationship, but he's also prone to taking off for days without telling us, and then there are the constant sidelong comments that make it clear he's never too happy about what he does to help us out, just that he feels he has to. And maybe he has a point. It's not like my mom or I have ever volunteered to arrange our own supply of blood.

"See you soon," I mutter into the phone, then turn back to the road.

The desert sun is hard at work by the time I pull into Uncle Bill's cul-de-sac, the exposure-scorched sidewalks and cracked asphalt driveways radiating such relentless heat that the air almost shimmers with it. His white stucco one-story is layered with world-weary grime that can only be achieved through years of dedication to subminimal maintenance. Instead of a row of palms or an Astroturf lawn out front, it's just a patch of dirt that the neighbor's dogs consistently shit in. Even though they clean up after, it still smells foul to me. Probably does to Uncle Bill too. I don't know how he stands it.

I find him out back, folded into a faded lawn chair in the shadow of the house. The back isn't any nicer than the front, more parched concrete and an empty pool collecting layers of dead tree bits and dirt.

His knees crack like a pair of snapped branches as he hauls himself to his feet. "You got here fast."

There's a certain youthfulness to Uncle Bill, even though he walks slower these days and his hair's thinning and mostly gray. He has the same nose as my mom, narrow and high bridged with a bump in the middle, and he reeks of drugstore cologne turned rancid by sweat and too many cups of instant coffee. Beneath that lurks the vinegary chemical stink of detergent and Windex that's so sunk into his hands that it'll never leave, no matter how many times he washes them.

Uncle Bill is a custodian at the UNLV phlebotomy lab. That's the reason we came here. My mom was tired of drifting and scheming, of digging through hazardous waste bins for trashed Vacutainers and raiding med-spa dumpsters for the discard of their vampire facials. Doesn't matter that it's been processed, or that it might have pathogens. If it's blood, it can't hurt us, only feed us. Medical samples are best, she taught me, because a standard three-milliliter vial is about what we need for a day. And we don't drink it, ever—drinking blood is wasteful and inconsistent, since a mouthful doesn't always damp our hunger for the same amount of time, depending on what food's in our stomach. Injection's clean, easy. Safe.

"There's coffee in the kitchen," Uncle Bill says. "Go pop the hood, will you?"

A dried-out branch snaps. Dirt slides deeper into the pool's concrete embrace.

I shuffle out front and open up my car. It takes me two tries to get the prop rod stable under the hood. Down the street, someone's watering their lemon tree. The smell of it suffuses the dust in the air, delicate, not too sweet, and out of nowhere I imagine my mouth filling with the lemony slick of Zawadski's—Veer's—hair gel.

My hands in her hair, my mouth on her neck, the aftertaste of citrus, sweat, and eager fascination.

"What the fuck," I whisper to the sun. Maybe if I stare at it long enough, it'll burn the image right out of my brain. When that doesn't work, I get busy pulling the dead battery out of the car.

Uncle Bill joins me after a minute. He scrubs coffee residue from his front teeth before wiping his hands on his jeans. "You know your mom's full of shit, don't you, Ellie?"

I never liked being called Ellie, but my mom made me swear I'd never correct him. "Nice way to talk about your sister."

"You know I'm right." He hoists the new battery over the edge of the bumper. "Want some advice?"

"No."

"Quit letting her ruin your life." The battery clicks into place. "Don't tell me she's not. She runs you around in circles, always has. What is it, you think you have something to prove to her?"

"She needs me," I say automatically.

"No, what she needs is—"

"She needs us."

He grips the hood and guides the prop rod back into its slot. "You know, if it was just her, I wouldn't be bothering. She can make her own way. But there was you too. So maybe try thinking for yourself for once."

A little black-and-white dog scampers past us, snuffles in the dirt of Uncle Bill's front yard, and cocks his leg.

"Hey! Rudy!" A woman in neon workout gear sprints up behind the dog and whisks him into her arms just before his bladder gets going.

"Oh my god, I'm so sorry," she says to Uncle Bill. Her blond ponytail has the copper undertones of a home bleach job. "I don't know why he does that."

"It's fine. Have a good one."

She jogs off, Rudy at her heels, and Uncle Bill gives me a look like *And you think you have problems.*

"What do you want me to do?" I hiss. "Stick her in a home I can't afford, where they don't know how to take care of whatever we are, and wait until she turns inside out and devours everyone in the place?"

"That's not the only option."

"You think I should kill her?"

He shrugs. "You tell me."

"No," I say quickly. "Fuck no. What's wrong with you?"

Our wounds heal, because that's the only way to survive with hunger ready to rip through you if you leave it too long. Our minds don't. If one of us goes that way, lucidity and reason fading out before their body does, it's the role of the next generation to slide a kitchen knife or a camping stake or a rusted machete through their loved one's chest, to release them from the torture of appetite. But I still see flashes of my mom, the real her, in between the bouts of confusion and anguish, and I can't help hoping.

Uncle Bill drops the hood closed with a bang. "Quit acting like you're the center of the universe. There are other people going through it too."

"Okay." Not like this. Not like us.

"No, there—" Instead of finishing, he wipes his hands again on the dirty rag and tosses it toward the garage. He's been around my mom and me long enough to know when something's a lost cause, I guess. "Whatever, not like you ever listen anyway. At least try to have some fun when she's not around."

Easy for him to say. I chose this. I went to nursing school because it gave me options: I could have picked anywhere in the country and found a decent-paying job with plausible access to blood. I could have survived away from my family, but there's a need for them somewhere in me that's beyond survival. And there's a debt. For that need, and that debt, I let my dreams of independence go when my mom stopped just forgetting where she put her keys and started forgetting what day it was, when to turn off the stove. And it's not forever. When she's gone . . .

Don't. I owe my mom. I'm not sure what, maybe love, maybe obedience, certainly my time and my care and the good fucking attitude I can't ever seem to scrape together. Giving her anything but my all would be the same as abandoning her.

"I'm only saying it because I love you," Uncle Bill adds. On the next street over, someone revs a leaf blower.

"Okay, so then why—"

Uncle Bill pats his pockets and produces his phone. I can't hear it ringing over the leaf blower, but he grimaces. "Gotta take this."

Of course he does. This is why I'm the one taking care of my mom, not him. He'll help us, begrudgingly, but he's never been interested in being responsible for anyone but himself. If I left things up to him, he'd look for the quick way out. He'd reach for the knife.

"Bill here," he says into the phone, his voice brash and businesslike. But the bravado doesn't make it as far as his face. He looks disappointed, and like there's something else he'd rather say, but he knows better than to say it. He tucks the phone into the angle of his chin and whispers, "Grab something out of the garage before you go, okay?"

That's another thing about Uncle Bill. He never likes to say *blood.*

He turns back to the phone, and I head for the garage door, but he pulls me back in by the shoulder, not demanding, just a little solemn, and kisses the top of my head. Like he used to when I was in high school, when I'd roll my eyes, thinking I was too old for it. Like he used to, apparently, to my mom, when they were kids.

"Thanks," I mutter. I'm not quite sure what I'm thanking him for.

The temperature of the air drops as I let myself into the garage. The single light bulb dangling over the door flickers awake. Uncle Bill's truck looms over me, a hulking black pickup with tinted windows and a bumper sticker that reads *I DON'T HAVE ROAD RAGE, YOU'RE JUST AN IDIOT.* I step carefully around the tangle of power tools and paint buckets discarded in a heap on the floor. It smells like concrete and cold in here, like spilled beer and spent shells and other things I don't really want to look at too closely.

Except for the massive stainless steel freezer humming in one corner. That smells like blood.

I pull a plastic bag from atop the freezer, line it with cold packs, and wedge the vials gently in among the crevices. They've still got stickers on them, some of the names smudged where they pressed up against melting ice. I try to avoid reading them—it feels like an invasion of privacy. I wonder if any of these people imagined this was where their samples would end up when they sat down with the phlebotomist.

I take enough for a week.

Uncle Bill's gone when I come back out, probably in the back saying things I don't want to hear into his phone. It's another part of our unspoken agreement with him: he feeds us, and we don't ask him who his friends are or how he managed to buy a house on a custodian's salary.

The leaf blower is still going, its rumble adding a layer of discomfort to just standing still. Halfway home, I realize that the song I switched on to drown it out got stuck somehow, and it keeps repeating, over and over, the same swell of triumph, the same downward inflection, the same chorus of disappointment.

4

MY MOM'S WATCHING *NIGHT COURT* AND DOING HER nails when I come in. On the screen, Judge Harry Stone ogles a beauty queen in a witch hat and bad wig. My mom leaps up, and half a set of checkerboard press-ons cascades to the floor.

"Hi, Mom." I nod at the plastic bag dangling from my hand. "Let me get these into the freezer."

Her face crumples, and she slinks back to her seat. Onscreen, the clerk shouts, "Why didn't you use a knife?"

Through the fuzzy TV speakers, the canned laughter sounds especially hollow.

"How's your morning?" I ask as I pry the slippery cold packs free. The apartment is laid out in the shape of a T, living room and kitchen mashed together in the front, our two bedrooms and a bathroom in a row in the back, with beige walls and laminate flooring that looked slick when we moved in but has since deformed at the seams. Constellations of Post-its crawl across the walls, the door, the countertops, like neon cicadas waiting for dusk. *Can opener in here* stuck on one drawer in vivid pink. *Wash hands before eating!* next to the sink in eye-watering orange.

The books I read suggested I show her old photo albums, ask her for old stories, force her to keep a grip on her memories by repeating them out loud. But we have no photos in the living room, and my mom has never been one to dwell on the past. Most of her stories end in disappointment.

"My nails," she moans. "They're all over the floor."

"I'll get them in a second. Are you hungry?"

"I don't know."

The ice machine spits out a few forlorn cubes as I wedge the vials into the corner of the freezer. They teeter on top of stacked bags of frozen vegetables, but I can fix that later. Right now, I need to focus on my mom. It's a delicate thing, judging whether she's actually incapable or just demanding things of me because she knows she can. It changes day to day. Maybe she really is overwhelmed by something so small. The knotty edge of the living room carpet digs into my knees as I scoop the scattered nails into her waiting hands.

"Let me do it for you," I say.

"Do what?"

"The blood. If you're hungry."

She frowns. "You know, baby, I nearly passed out when I had you, not from the pain but from the sight of all that blood."

When I look at her, the brown flecks in her eyes seem swollen against her gray-green irises. Her face is slightly slack, her expression vacant.

"I'll be right back," I promise her. "I'll take care of everything."

My mom isn't afraid of blood. You can't be, with a hunger

like ours. But I don't mind her lying about it, because it's something she always claimed, all my life. Means she's still in there, somewhere.

The truth is that I was born in the bathroom of a Motel 6 on the side of the highway between Lawrence and Topeka, Kansas, and from that moment I was my mom's best friend, her safeguard, her identity. Her family left her by degrees, her father first, left a corpse as her mother sped away on the interstate, then Uncle Bill hitting the road when she was in elementary school, and finally, her mother disappearing on a sweltering June night, her only goodbye a scrawled note of *I can't do it anymore, be good, I love you.* All those abandonments carved a hole in my mom's heart, and my reason for existing was to fill it.

The truth is, too, that we were each born with ribs suffused with iron, and a need for blood each day to keep the prison of our bones intact. Only that blood and that cage and our will keeps hunger from invading our bodies and devouring everything before us.

"Once, when man was just another animal" is how my mom began the story of what we are. Before I remember anything else, I remember her voice, telling it. "The flayed god crouched at the edge of time and sanity, and breathed life into a blade of iron. It grew arms and legs and a snout and teeth. So many teeth. It was our ancestor, but unlike us, it couldn't control its hunger."

She'd brush the tiny floating hairs back from my forehead, her touch light, tender. Loving.

"One by one, men fell before its appetite. Until, at last, it came to the home of a great warrior. 'A curse upon you!' the warrior cried as he, too, met death at the jaws of the monster.

But that didn't matter, because the creature was already cursed.

"As it finished devouring the great warrior, the warrior's daughter emerged. She howled, not a howl of vengeance but a howl of gratitude. The warrior had kept his daughter like a prisoner all her life and now she was free. Even with her father's blood still dripping from its muzzle, she loved this terrible thing. It did not know language, so she spoke to it in the only way she could: with a knife pressed over her heart."

My mom tapped that same place in my chest, showing me just where my own monster hid.

"The creature stilled its rampage. With its long black tongue, it licked her wound clean, and from her blood it gained the power of speech. It cut the skin from one of its victims and stepped into it and became a man. And so the monster and the warrior's daughter became a family, and they taught their children how to keep safe from their hunger so they would never devour those they loved."

No one becomes like us. You're either born human or born hungry. And no one can ever understand me, can ever love me down to my bones and the snarling beast beyond like family can.

I lay out a fresh syringe and numbing wipe side by side on the counter. The vials defrosted enough on the drive here to be liquid inside, despite the cold packs.

"Roll your sleeve up, Mom," I call over my shoulder.

She wiggles around, head hanging over the armrest. "What's up with you? Are you mad at me?"

"Just roll up your sleeve. You pick which arm."

I fill up the syringe. When I turn around, she's pushed both sleeves up above the elbow.

She relaxes at the sight of the needle. It's instinct after a lifetime of need, even as she asks, frowning with confusion, "What's that for?"

I crouch next to her. "How about your right arm?"

She nods and offers it up.

When I was a kid, my mom only ever held my hand in public. She'd scoop me up and perch me on her hip, leaning in to charm the other parents, to tell them how fast I was learning—*and already growing her adult teeth!* But when it was just the two of us, there was always a distance. Between the daughter she wanted and the person I was. A distance I tried every day, every month, every year to close, and always failed. Now, when I trace the spidering lines of her veins with my thumb, a private highway traversing the tender underside of her forearm, she smiles a small, secret smile and closes her eyes. When the needle breaks her skin, she squeezes my hand so tight it's like she's trying to fuse us together.

"What would I do without you, Ellis?" she mumbles, eyes still closed, her dark hair fanned out over the back of the chair, the gray threads in it glittering like stars.

My throat catches, and I can't get out a reply. So I retreat to dig under the sink for the empty detergent bottle we use for old syringes. She murmurs something else I don't catch.

"What was that?" The syringe clatters into the orange plastic expanse. On the TV, the Brooklyn Bridge zooms into focus, grainy and overbright.

"You're not going to get rid of me, are you?"

"No, Mom, of course not." The screen fades back into the make-believe courtroom. I sink down to kneel at her feet. "I love you."

"Love you too." She strokes a hand through my hair, and

suddenly I'm desperate to have the long, silky, elegant hair she always wanted for me, not this half-grown-out bob left stringy after a long night. This is the real her, who remembers, who whispers her gratitude, who tells me she loves me. Maybe it's all been a misunderstanding, maybe today is when we'll really feel like mother and daughter, maybe it'll all start to be easy. I'll grow my hair out, I'll start taking better care of myself, I'll find something to wear that I didn't buy in college. I won't have to fight to remember what's real and what's not.

She pats my hair again, and my scalp tingles with hope.

"Are you going to work already?" she asks. Her gaze isn't on me, but the scuffed sneakers still on my feet. "I want some more of that bread from the Colombian bakery. The one on Sahara. You don't mind getting it while you're out, do you?"

Oh, that's right. Hope is for other people.

"Sure, Mom." I fix my eyes on the cracks in the ceiling. "Right after I shower."

It's an old trick. By the time I finish showering, she'll forget that she asked.

As the water runs, I thrust my awareness inward, groping past my sternum and around the slimy curves of my lungs until I find a beast on an iron chain. I whistle softly. Its dark-furred ears perk up. It strains against the pitted curves of its prison.

I trace the cold, sure edges of this cage that is my heart. My skin prickles with savage excitement, with the possibility of throwing the lock and letting the creature inside me run. How would it feel to embrace all my pent-up violence, to let the viciousness soaked through me have its way? I'm not so stupid as to give in to that temptation. But sometimes it soothes me to place my fingers within snapping distance of the sharp jaws of my ferocity. It's the only time I'm sure that I'm real.

A text from Uncle Bill pops up on my phone as I'm drying my hair.

Stay safe, it reads. *Both of you.*

I text back, *Don't we always*, with a smiley face. It's hard to know what these things mean with him. Maybe he read something fucked up in the *Review-Journal*. Three dots appear, vanish, reappear, as he types, deletes, types again.

We will, I add quickly. I want to get to bed, not have a drawn-out text conversation. *Thanks. Love you.*

There is no safety for us, not really. We choose between scheming and stealing to get the blood we need, or a brief brutal burst as a monster. We tell kids that the flayed man can only smell us when we're transformed, that he's always hunting, always hoping, but as long as we stay human, we're safe from him—we tell kids that, because the truth is scarier. If I got so hungry my bones came through my skin, it wouldn't be the flayed man who killed me. It would be a cop or a guard or some other guy with a gun, and he'd be right to do it, because once we transform, there's nothing left but destruction.

We have stories about that too. Abandoned infants who become killing machines, mothers whose jaws slip loose from their sheathes. Teenagers testing their limits, put down by a bullet.

I crawl into bed, the sun slashing slivers of brightness around the edges of the curtains, and do my best to forget it all.

5

THE NEXT FEW DAYS ARE A BLUR OF WORK AND WORRY and my mom's entreaties. I stop at the Colombian bakery and get the bread she likes. Just one loaf, but my stomach sours as I get into my car, and I end up going back for a second. She swallows her daily pills, a round one the color of Dijon mustard and an oblong one the color of cooked chicken breast, while I hold out a glass of water and feign disinterest. It humiliates her, any sign that I don't trust her to manage it herself, even if we both know that I don't. I order takeout and we watch reruns of *L.A. Law.* I sleep when I can. Someone's grandfather comes into the hospital with a burst appendix. A twenty-year-old in labor who didn't know she was pregnant, a man with a bullet through his foot, ruined sneaker and ruined flesh so intermingled they became something new, no longer separate.

My mom seems all right, until she doesn't.

I'm heading to work. She's supposed to be napping. I run

the dishwasher and start scratching away at a fresh Post-it. *I'm at work, be back by 6. Love you, Ellis.*

A door slams, slicing through the whir of the dishwater. The pen flies out of my hand and rolls somewhere under the couch.

"Ellis." Her voice is thick with sleep. The old T-shirt she sleeps in sags off one shoulder. "Someone's in the house."

I'm almost electrocuted with panic, until I see what she's got in her hand: a bright pink Post-it. Even with her thumb covering the middle, I recognize my own handwriting. *Hair-brush is in the second drawer to the right.*

"I wrote that." It comes out too harsh. My skin crawls in the electric current's aftermath. "It's for you. To help you."

She frowns and pats at her hair. The frizzy halo goes lop-sided. "You wrote it?"

"Yes, Mom." Don't say it too fast, or it'll sound like an ad-mission of guilt. Don't say it too slow, or she'll accuse me of talking down to her. "I write all of them."

Her eye catches one of the Post-its stuck to the wall. *Keep the thermostat at 70.* Her frown draws lines like railroad tracks between her features. She scans the living area, where more Post-its scatter the coffee table—*Green button = on, Red button = off*—the TV—*Don't unplug!*—the side of the fridge, the counters, the walls.

"Why would you write these?" Her voice arcs up, high pitched and pitiful. "Do you think I'm stupid?"

"Of course not, it's—"

Too slow. She rushes from note to note, crumpling them up and tossing them wildly. Post-its flutter around the room like a flurry of multicolored snow. "You do, don't you. I've never been good enough for you. Does bossing me around make you feel good? Does it make you feel special?"

"I'm just trying to help."

She snatches a cereal box off the counter and flings it to the ground. Cornflakes scatter like ashes. "I don't need your help. I can take care of myself."

"No, you can't," I snap. No, remember all the books, all the advice. Stay calm. Don't argue. But it's too late now. "You forget things. You're going to hurt yourself or someone else if I don't write the notes. I'm not—it's not—I'm just trying to make sure you're okay."

Her mouth twists into a pout. "Everyone forgets things. Remember when you forgot your homework at that rest stop in Colorado and we had to drive an extra three hours to get it?"

She's brought that up a hundred times, when we have this very same argument. Only for her, every time still feels like the first.

"This is different."

"Different?" She kicks at the cereal carnage around her. "Different how?"

I open my mouth, but she's back on the offense. "I'll tell you how it's different. It's different because you want it to be different. He's poisoning your mind. He's trying to take you away from me. Just like he took my mother."

In her worst moments, my mom is her sixteen-year-old self again, searching for meaning in her mother's abandonment. If her mother had been kidnapped, had been devoured by a monster, had been murdered and dumped on the side of the road, even, she might sleep better at night, because that would mean her mother hadn't simply walked away.

"Mom, your mother—"

"I know what you're going to say!" she screeches. "I know what you're going to say, but that's just what he makes you think!" She sweeps a deafening cascade of silverware from the dish rack to the floor. "The flayed man, he watches me! He's waiting!"

Plates and bowls follow the silverware. My ears ring with bright flares of crashing melamine. My mom's alone at night when I work, and most of the day while I sleep. The flayed man is imaginary, but what if someone *is* watching her?

Before I can collect myself, she shifts her attention to the fridge.

"I'm hungry," she whines, tugging at the door. All of the rage bleeds out of her in a second. So fast that if I'm not careful, I'll start to wonder if it was ever there at all.

"Mom." I try to control the worry seeping into my voice. It might be nothing. She gets paranoid sometimes, and she was already agitated over the Post-its. "Has anyone but me and Joanne come into the apartment?"

Joanne is our upstairs neighbor, who drops by every so often to help scrub the shower or clean out the fridge. She's the person my mom calls if she needs something while I'm at work.

"No." She pulls the fridge door open, then slams it closed again with a dull thud. "Stop being dramatic."

"But you said—"

My mom juts her lower lip out, childlike. "Well, I made that up."

"You—" I can't tell if my disbelief is real or just another form of frustration. "Why?"

"You were being a brat."

Something in my gut untwists. We're back on familiar ground now. We've played this game before, my mom and me.

"Okay." I pick through the kitchen shrapnel scattered on

the floor and stretch across her, reaching for the freezer. "Let me get you something to eat."

She beats me to it, wrenching the freezer door open with all her strength. Impact rings in my ears, and my vision shatters into a haze of sparks. By the time I put together what's happened—she opened the freezer door right into my face, *fuck*—I'm already sagging against the sink. I brace myself on one elbow and shake my head to clear the explosion away.

A thump, and ice chips skitter across the kitchen floor. Another, heavier, the sodden cardboard of a microwave meal landing on its side. I catch a bag of frozen peas, toss them into the sink, but miss another bag of corn that hits the ground with a slap.

"Ellis?" My mom wavers. Under it I hear the clear command: *Fix this.*

I think of Uncle Bill, and the heartless way he urged me to live for myself. My mom can barely feel her way around a syringe some days, and cries in the shower because she confuses the hot and cold. What would she do without my Post-its, my reminders, my assurances, my sacrifices?

She'd be devoured by the curse in her heart, and no sacrifice, no patience, no love is enough to stop it once it's jumped its chain. So my mom will die quietly, her mind run out on her, and I'll put a kitchen knife through her ribs to separate her from her hunger. Until then, I'm tied to her. She needs me.

A shattering noise wrenches me back to the present. Then, the smell. Blood like nitrile gloves and rubber coating, like chemical heartburn, like loneliness.

Another vial rolls over the lip of the freezer and smashes on the linoleum. It smells like hope, like need. My mom is on her knees, hands thrust into the leakage, lifting a ruddy mess of glass and ice to her mouth. Red drips through her fingers, melting where it meets skin, splattering her pajama shirt.

"Mom." I kneel next to her, wrap my arms around her wrists. I need to secure the remaining vials, but I need to help her first, before she swallows those slivers of glass into places I can't fish them out. "Mom, put that down."

She bucks against my grip. "Mom, listen to me. There's glass in there. Put your hands down, and I'll get you a fresh vial."

Glass on plastic, rolling. Another one shatters. She twists, trying to snatch for it, and growls a sound that scrapes warning down my spine.

"Mom!" She whips around, and her lips are pulled back, canines glinting too large, the tongue behind them blackening and something primal and ghastly menacing me through her eyes.

Then it's gone. She relaxes. She lets me maneuver her to the sink to shake the glass from her clenched fists and flush clean the lacerations made by that fistful of sharpened points. My temple stings. It's going to bruise. I'd better come up with something good to tell my supervisor about that, and about being late. But if I hadn't snapped at her, if I hadn't imposed, if I hadn't stacked the vials so precariously . . .

I know it's not my fault. But it's still my responsibility to fix it.

I scrub the floor and stack the dishes and return the frozen vegetables to their rightful places. I change out of my blood-soaked pants, settle my mom in front of the couch, and turn on *The Golden Girls*. I call my supervisor as I fumble with my car keys and explain in a breathless rush, unable to pause even as she talks over me, assuring me it's okay, it's okay, it's okay.

It's not okay. It's getting worse every day.

I call Uncle Bill as I drive, the highway howling outside my cracked-open window. Tell him I need to come by again, that something's happened. I can't bring myself to explain the specifics, but I think he guesses.

"Sure, Ellie." He hacks out a cough. Maybe hard living's finally catching up to him. "Want to come by now?"

"I'm late for work. Can I come in the morning?"

"Sure thing. If I'm out, you know how to get into the garage."

"Thanks."

"Anytime. Don't work too hard."

I laugh, but it sounds fake. Feels fake too. Maybe he hears it, because he says, suddenly, "You can't put it off forever, you know."

"Put what off?" I don't feel like laughing anymore.

"I don't know." But he does, and I do too. He means stirring some Xanax into her tea and letting her fall asleep forever. Driving her out to the desert and ripping her throat out with my fangs. "Life's a bitch."

Yeah, or maybe bitterness is just the cost of living like we do. Just because he's family doesn't mean he knows me, what I'm capable of, what I can do or what I can stand.

"See you in the morning, Uncle Bill." I hang up, resisting the urge to hurl my phone out of the window to blow away into the desert's waiting maw like just another tumbleweed.

A long night of busted noses and sliced-off fingers cools my frustration. By the time I pull into Uncle Bill's driveway, I'm almost hoping he's awake early again, that he'll offer me a cup of his nasty instant coffee, that he'll apologize or commiserate or, I don't know. It's a little disappointing to find the door locked and all the lights off.

The garage is cold, like always.

His truck is gone, so he must be out. Everything looks normal, cables and power tools and paint buckets, but the smell is wrong. Subtly, at first, an unexpected sterile edge to the air. The closer I get to the freezer, the more it presses in on me, the sense that something's off. Something's missing.

I flip the heavy lid up. A pale tundra of ice chips and humming insulation stares back. The freezer's empty.

"Fuck." Uncle Bill really couldn't be bothered to restock the freezer before he left? Or at least tell me to come by later? Is this some kind of sick punishment for disagreeing with him about my mom?

There's a dark stain in the corner. The remnants of a smashed vial, slivers of glass stabbing up through the tattered label like glittering teeth through black-and-white gums. I drop the lid, and the slam of foam on plastic rings fuzzy in my ears. I press my thumbs into the space between my eyeballs and brow bones until my vision doubles, then quadruples, then goes black.

When I open my eyes next, the walls are dripping blood. Red runs from the seams in the wood, foams up from the cracks in the cement, dotted with twisting white worms.

Then I blink, and the walls are clean.

God, Ellis. Get it together. A trick of the half-dead fluorescent bulbs, or an afterimage of pressing my thumbs into my eyes. Uncle Bill probably tripped over one of the stupid coiling cables and broke some vials. That's so like him, to say he's got my back and then forget to follow through. So what?

That's why the truck is gone, he left early for work to replace the blood he ruined.

But when I try to swallow, a pebble of uncertainty rattles through my esophagus, past my stomach, my intestines, and settles like a lead weight in my feet.

Hey man, I text him before pulling out of the driveway, *you could have told me the freezer was empty*. Then I feel guilty and add, *Is tomorrow morning okay? I can bring takeout or something.*

My mom's asleep on the couch when I get home. I take an extra-long shower and unload the dishwasher, then crawl into bed, set my alarm, and try not to be too pissed at Uncle Bill for letting me down.

I dream about a faceless ghost in a medic jacket, and the smell of lemons. I wake up to screaming.

6

I BOLT OUT OF MY BEDROOM TO FIND JOANNE SILHOUETTED in the door and my mom in front of her, brandishing a wooden spoon.

"Get out!" she shrieks.

Joanne clutches the doorjamb, her quilted vest dangling off her gaunt frame. She's in her sixties, withered by decades of faith in the goodness of the world, faith that's constantly disappointed.

Her son died last year. Blew his own face off. An accident, Joanne says, cleaning his gun and didn't realize it was loaded, but who knows. She doesn't see much of her grandkids.

I want to like Joanne, but I don't.

She shoots a pleading look at me over my mom's shoulder, and the automatic assumption that my mom can't or won't listen to her grates, even if it's true. Give her some fucking autonomy, Joanne. I can smell the swollen, tender pieces of your organs, the fluid building up where it shouldn't. It's not like you're the peak of health.

"Hey, Mom," I say, soft and soothing. "Let me talk to her."

My mom's shoulder's sag. The wooden spoon bangs against her thigh. "I'm sorry," I mutter to Joanne, and fish in my purse for the eighty dollars I owe her. She wants to take it, I can tell, but she still makes a show of protesting until I insist and insist and insist. As she leaves, I smell pity on her breath.

"What happened?" I ask my mom after the door clicks shut. She's slumped into the couch, thumb idly tracing the corner of the TV remote.

"The flayed man called me." She sounds like herself, clear and sure. "He said he visited Bill. He said he's still hungry. Then Joanne knocked on the door, and I got scared."

"So you yelled?"

"Yeah."

"But you kept yelling. You woke me up."

A childlike craftiness gleams in her eyes. "I wanted her to leave."

"Okay." Uncle Bill must have called to apologize or explain about the missing blood. She's just confused or telling me whatever she thinks will get her the most sympathy. "About the call. Did he leave a message?"

"He said Bill's an asshole and he's going to leave us." Her words begin to run together. "Can't let him. I can't . . . be good. We need . . ."

I settle onto the couch next to her. The cushions bend so much more under my weight than hers. She forgets to eat, sometimes, if I don't remind her.

"I mean, yeah, Mom, Uncle Bill comes and goes, but he always comes back. You're sure it wasn't him who called?"

She crosses her arms, thinking. "Maybe. You know I get confused."

"I know. It's okay. When you said yesterday that someone was watching you, were you confused then too?"

"No." She frowns. "You know who he is." She makes claws of her hands and gestures to her chest, the way she used to when I was a kid and she told me stories during the long late-night drives. "He says Bill is going to leave, and you're going to leave, and then it'll be just me and him and his hungry jaws."

Her words slur, and she blinks slowly, like she's exhausted. Or like she's not sure of what she'll find when she opens her eyes.

"I'm not going to leave," I assure her. I reach for her hand, but she flinches away, her face going suddenly wooden.

"You're not going to leave?"

Something's wrong, but I can't quite tell what. "Of course not."

She pushes herself upright, shoulders squared. "You can't just barge in here. My daughter's coming home any minute."

My stomach drops.

"Mom." My voice betrays me, shaking a little as I round out the word. "Who do you think I am?"

"Stop trying to confuse me." She twists away, burying her face in the couch cushion. Her words come out muffled by polyester. "Just leave me alone."

"Okay." God, this hurts. Every time, so much that I promise myself the next time has to be easier. And it never is. "I'll be in the other room."

Usually that's enough. But not tonight. Tonight, she whips forward and spits, "Get out of my house."

It's not your house, I want to retort. I pay the damn rent. Instead, I say, "How about you watch something on TV?"

"Get out." She rockets upright, leaning hard on the arm of the chair. "Get out! Intruder!"

I know what comes next if I fight her on this. She goes for a knife, or she bangs on the wall, and the night ends in screams and sobs and apologies to the neighbors.

"Okay." I grab my coat, shuffle my purse onto my shoulder. "I'll go. I'm leaving."

The door shuts and the dead bolt clicks, and I slump my forehead into the cold metal of our apartment numbers. These are the times when it feels like wading through mud just to remember what's real and what's not.

What's real is that the door is locked. I have the keys in my purse, but going back inside will only make things worse. What's real is that my options are to spend a couple of hours curled pathetically on my own doorstep or find somewhere else to go.

I push the edge of my house key into the pad of my thumb and try calling Uncle Bill. He doesn't pick up. I feel like a sieve, all my strength escaping out the holes poked through me. I just want to escape too.

Fuck it. I'll go to Rosy's.

There aren't many lesbian bars in Vegas. Actually, there aren't any, just a couple of bars where lesbians hang out sometimes, and Rosy's is the shittiest one. But it's close enough to walking distance, and it feels good to be cocooned by the roar of cars and the mutter of fast-food drive-through speakers and the piss-and-trash smell of the sidewalk.

Wedged between a smoke shop, its windows advertising *Pipes! Hookah! Cigars!* in gloating gold letters, and an insurance agency with boarded-up windows, Rosy's is empty inside except for a skinny couple in the corner, with their heads together. They both have the exact same shade of dark-brown, almost-black hair. A soccer game flickers on the TV, showering distorted cheers over the scarred leather of a vacant booth.

The bar smells like Pine-Sol and maraschino cherries. I order a Coke. The bartender leaves that hanging in the air with a look of expectation, so I change it to a rum and Coke. It leaves a sugary film on my tongue. When I'm done, I order another one.

"Waiting for a friend?" The bartender asks. The tattoos on her knuckles spell out *HOLD FAST ♡ DIE LAST.*

"Just waiting."

A couple of bodies fill in the barstools between me and the door. I play with my phone while the bartender pours beers and asks about weekend plans.

"I took my wife to the new Italian spot on the Strip," she says, when someone turns the question back on her. A glass appears in her hand, thunks down on the plastic mat.

"Special occasion?"

"Anniversary. Fifteen years." She stretches out the *teen* like a piece of bubblegum.

"Congrats."

"Not to my wallet." She chuckles. "Twenty dollars for a martini. I can make a better martini with my eyes closed!" When the patron laughs appreciatively, she adds, "Good thing it's 'till death do us part,' not 'till bankruptcy,' am I right?"

Then the door swings open, and I smell lemons.

Her hair's slicked back, same way it was when she jumped my car, but now instead of the medic jacket, she's got on baggy jean shorts, a white tank top hacked off above the belly button, and definitely no bra.

"Tequila!" Veer howls and swings herself onto an open stool at the opposite end of the bar. The movement tugs her hip free of her waistband, and the neon hum of the Budweiser sign above the bar catches on the faint line of a healed cut. Something in me lurches.

I don't want her to see me like this, alone and miserable. Especially since she came with friends, a Southeast Asian girl with sleeve tattoos and a million facial piercings, and a pasty stick of a person with a big sharp nose and hair that's brown at the roots and green at the ends. I watch out of the corner of my eye as the bartender splashes out three tequila shots. Veer drums her middle finger against the bar, impatient, and I wonder what it would feel like trapped between my teeth.

I need to get the fuck out of here.

I get the bartender's attention and pay my tab. Veer's back is to me. Her hand flicks up to fuss with her already-well-smudged eyeliner, at the same time her neighbor on the left—not one of her friends, some guy in faded brown leather—turns his head. Her elbow catches him squarely on the chin.

I shrink back into my seat.

"Excuse me?" The guy sounds pissed. I guess I would be too, getting an abrupt elbow to the face like that.

"Shit." Veer peers at him, getting in his space a little. "I'm sorry, man, I didn't mean to. Can I—"

He doesn't wait for her to finish, just turns back to his drink, and I only know he says something else because Veer bristles. She steps off her stool, her mouth a stubborn line. The air caramelizes like the scorched aftertaste of an electric shock, the dead calm before a hurricane, the tension before the first swing of a fight.

Shit.

I don't care if Veer gets into it with some guy. I don't care about her at all. Focus on getting out of here, on going home and nursing my misery. Ignore the smell of spilled beer and soda-sweet breath and walk out the door.

Except when the guy stands, I see the waist holster. Veer's really in his face now, one of her friends whispering desperately in her ear, trying to pull her away, while the other one hurriedly slides over cash for their shots.

The bartender slams her palm on the bar. "Chill out or take it outside."

Veer shrugs off her friend's concern. "I'm chill."

"It's fine," the guy growls. "I'm out of here."

The door swings wide as he shoves through it, and Veer pushes through her friends to go after him. That's fine. That's good. I didn't want her to see me, and now she won't.

But she helped you with your car, an intolerable urge hisses. You may not owe her much for that, but you at least owe her this.

I make it to the door about a half step before she does. She doesn't quite stop, tries to shoulder me out of the way before she recognizes me. I can trace the red lines of exhaustion in the whites of her eyes.

"I know you," she says, painfully loud. "You work at Sunrise. I jumped your car."

"Yeah." Adrenaline makes all my fine motor movements too large, too sudden. "Hey, don't go after him. It's not worth it."

Her glare burrows into the hollow center of my chest. I want to bite into the softness of her throat, want to feel my claws on her skin and her tongue in my mouth. I want, I want, I want.

No. Not here. Not her. That's the kind of thing to bury deep, because even glancing at it might tip me off the edge of the world and leave me for drowning.

"Veer, you stupid bitch," one of her friends screeches, and right, I'm in a bar and there are other people here, there's a whole world around me. But she's still staring.

"Ellis," she says quietly. "Right?"

I nod, and for one more electric second my curse and I both want the same thing.

"Let's go." The tattooed friend uncrosses her arms, and I see *Lavender Menace* scrawled across her shirt in big pink letters. "I paid our tab."

"You should come too," Veer says.

I shouldn't. I have too many issues of my own to get tied up in anyone else's.

"Are you paid up?" It's the other friend, the green-haired one, from over my shoulder.

I nod again, a little unwillingly.

"Then what's the holdup? Don't worry, she doesn't bite. Unless you're into that."

It would be heaven to have one night where I'm not at the mercy of my mom or a patient or anyone at all. To put aside all the shit I'm supposed to be dealing with and try to remember how to be alive. Have some fun, like Uncle Bill wanted. Don't I deserve that?

No, I don't. But those are just words, and the want's in my bones, and when Veer backs out the door, I find myself swept after her.

7

I LEARN THAT THE TATTOOED ONE IS KELSEY AND THE green-haired one is Lasso, and we're heading to someone's friend's old roommate's house party. Kelsey's car is clean enough, but there's a lingering smell of rancid oil and hot sauce.

In the passenger seat, Lasso kicks their sneakers up on the dashboard. "Vera. Veronica. Veruschka. We can't take you anywhere, girl."

Veer mutters, "Then don't."

"Be nice," Kelsey warns in her low gravel voice.

Lasso clicks their tongue. "Just saying."

Veer scrunches herself up against the door, forehead pressed into the window, and ignores them both.

Kelsey says something about a job interview, and Lasso giggles and folds forward and launches into a story. But there's a scent in the air, faint under the takeout-and-plastic odor of the car. Worry. Unspoken, unheeded. Kelsey is gripping the steering wheel so hard her knuckles blanch white.

Veer keeps her face to the window as we speed past flickering streetlights and neon-lit liquor stores. All the lights seem to be green.

A Chinese restaurant flies by in a flash of yellow and black, and Kelsey grumbles, "Worst fried rice of my life."

Lasso cackles. "Okay but, hear me out, have you ever been to this place downtown called Nice Restaurant #2? The fried rice there will drive you literally insane . . ."

Veer runs a palm over her skull, pushing her slicked-back hair even flatter. Did she only invite me along out of kindness? Was I supposed to say no? The headrest is tilted forward at a weird angle, and a meningitic stiffness has started to creep through my neck.

Fine. I'll say something.

"He had a gun." It sounded better when I was thinking it.

Veer doesn't shift, and I wonder if the words got lost in Lasso's chatter and the whir of rubber on asphalt. Then, right when I'm about to repeat myself, she shrugs herself around to face me and says, "Sure."

She flares her eyes as she says it, not quite an eye roll but the same idea. From the front, Kelsey hisses "Fuckin' dumbass" in a tone of flat, familiar warning that tells me it's meant for Veer, and beneath it is a whole continent of hurt and rage and fear.

"Okay," Veer says. "Okay, I'm a dumbass."

Up ahead, the light turns yellow. Kelsey speeds up. We fly through as the light blinks red. We cut through a gas station to avoid another red light, and Veer leans over to me so abruptly it looks stop-motion in the blue-white wash of the gas station lights.

"I'm sorry," she says under her breath, and I realize she

doesn't want her friends to hear. "I'm sorry again. I'm sorry I have to keep apologizing." The car bumps back onto the road, and she pulls away. "I'm a real fuckup, okay? Kels will tell you."

"She's a good kid," Lasso interjects. Veer punches the back of their headrest.

It's okay, I almost say, an automatic response. But I hold back, because what I want to say is: She loves you, your friend, I can hear it in her words, I can smell it on her breath. She loves you, and she's scared that one day she won't be able to pull you back from the edge. You don't know what I'd give to have someone care for me like that. Don't talk about her love with such bitterness.

In the end, I just smile and say nothing.

The car shudders to a stop outside a flat-roofed bungalow, pockmarked with grime blown in from the desert. The front yard is yellow grass crowned with a constellation of equally yellow plastic chairs, some upright and gathering dirt in their seats, some face down or knocked on one side like sad bowling pins. A pair of girls in frayed jeans and flannels lounge in the pushed-open window, legs flung over the sill for balance. As we approach, I smell Mountain Dew and the electric fuzz of appliances left plugged in as the house baked in the sun.

This isn't right—going to a party, going to *this* party, shutting the door on my mom and my problems for a night, even if she did shut the door on me first—but Veer turns around and slips her arm through mine, and I can't disengage now. Her skin is comfortingly cold, or maybe mine's just warm.

Veer drags me through the door, Veer who maybe can't stand me, or maybe wants something from me. Or maybe something kinder, but I never learned to look for the good in people. Past piles of purses and backpacks, sweatshirts flung on a side table, their arms twined together like an afterimage of an embrace. Inside, the lights are down and the music's up. Loose-limbed people fling themselves into and out of my field of vision, and Kelsey and Lasso disappear into the swirl.

"Let's get a drink," Veer whispers in my ear.

We maneuver over sprawled legs and around two figures in matching crop tops, making out in the hallway. The kitchen walls are a quilt of taped-up flyers, amateurish risograph prints, and Sharpie scrawls. Half-empty liquor bottles and beer cans litter the counter, flanked by abandoned plastic cups. Someone's doodled a floppy-eared dog and a speech bubbling reading "I love you!" on the nearest one.

Veer scans the bottles. "What do you like?" Her voice is loud and surprisingly close. "Tequila?"

"Sure."

She smacks her way through the forest of glass and plastic. The cup with the dog drawing topples onto its side with a mournful plop.

"What did he say to you?" I ask. "Back at the bar?"

Orange juice sloshes over the red lip of the cup. "Huh? Oh. Not, like, a slur, if that's what you're asking."

"No, I—" I'm suddenly off-kilter, not sure what to say. "I'm sorry. This is weird."

Veer's hands freeze midair. "For you?"

"No. For you. You don't have to—"

You don't have to do this, whatever this is. You don't have to spend all night with me just because you ran into me at a bar. Just because I'm still stinging from my mom's rejection doesn't mean you have to be gentle with me.

She doesn't know that, of course. About my mom. But that's not the point.

"Do I look like someone who does stuff because she has to?" She sneers and shoves a drink that smells like citrus and turpentine into my hand. "If you want to leave, go for it."

Her jaw is a tense line, her eyes dark rimmed and defiant. There's eyeliner on the bridge of her nose. I could reach up and wipe it away. I could cup her face in my hands and breathe her in. I could snarl my way into her bones.

A howl of laughter from some other room of the house. Veer breathes out, hard, the sure line of her pressed-together lips twisting. Not a smile. A grimace. Self-recrimination. She doubles over and digs her elbows into the tiled lip of the counter, slides her hands into her hair.

"Jesus," she mutters. "I'm sorry. Like, I know, I *know* I can be such a fucking freak show sometimes. No, don't be freaked out, it's seriously fine if you want to leave. You always look like you're, like, expecting a punch in the face, and I'm not that guy, I swear to God, I just. I don't know. I—" She slides her face into the crook of her elbow, muffling the rest.

It takes me a second to piece together what she's trying to say. "Like I'm—"

Her face pops up again. Her eyes are big, a little too big, like she's on the edge of panic. "Like you're expecting a punch in the face." Her voice, too, has a breathlessness, like now that she's started, she can't stop. "I see you all the time in the ED. That kid who shot himself in the leg, remember? And the guy who had a heart attack, with the wife who kept claiming she should do the CPR instead of me. And the lady who went into labor on the side of the road. And Oscar and Yvonne and the rest of our frequent flyers, and those kids who lost control of their bonfire, and—"

"And the mom who flipped her car," I finish for her, trying

not to remember her shaking hands as she bent over the little girl, her venom in the break room.

"No." That same venom is back, but fainter, softer, like sunlight filtered through a gauzy curtain. "You were different that time."

I *was* different. I was hungry.

She shakes her head, clearing a thought away maybe. The panic's gone. The venom too.

"Ellis." She makes my name sound like a full sentence. "Can I try again? Start over from the beginning?"

I nod. She steps closer. I suffocate on the smell of her curiosity, like anise and black pepper cracked between her molars.

"Okay. Good. Okay." A twitch of a smile, like she's nervous about letting it all the way onto her face. She tugs the cup from my hands and finishes it in one go. I imagine her tasting remnants of me amid the plastic and alcohol. "Wanna dance?"

The empty cup joins its brethren on the counter. "Yeah," I say. "Sure."

Veer holds out a hand and I take it, and then we're threading back toward the living room with its blaring speakers and twisting bodies. She walks fast, like she's worried that if we slow down, I'll change my mind. I remember the wailing wife, her insistence that she'd sue the medics for negligence. I remember the kids and the acrid smell of smoke. But I don't remember the others, and even if I did, I definitely don't remember which medics brought them in. But Veer noticed me, all those times. She remembered.

That shouldn't make me feel warm, but it does. Or maybe the two drinks I had at Rosy's are starting to get to me.

The living room is lit blue green by LED striplights,

punctuated by the glow of phone screens. The music roars and warps, going fuzzy where the song is too loud or too low for the cheap speakers to handle. We swerve around furniture shunted into corners to make way for unapologetic bodies, and Veer tugs me out of the way of a trio in combat boots and cartoon character backpacks who are shoving each other to the pump of the bass.

"Watch it." But she's smiling, like it's less a warning, more a suggestion. Watch them. Wouldn't that be fun?

In front of us, someone in a hot-pink T-shirt screeches and runs full tilt at someone else. They collapse to the floor together, a swamp of limbs and laughter.

"Shithead," Veer calls to them, and they swipe giddily at her ankles. Another partygoer tips head over heels as we pass, Doc Martens barely missing the back of Veer's skull.

"Are you sure—"

Her teeth flash, and she steers me toward the wall. "It's cool. I've got you."

The song switches, goes slower and sludgier, and Veer pushes her fingers into the spaces between mine until we're twined together, swaying. She leans in, so close I can smell the orange juice and cinnamon on her breath, and whispers something.

"What?"

She pulls back a bit. Repeats it, louder. "Ever been to a party like this before?"

"No." I'm sure she knew the answer before she asked the question.

She looks at me, and the air grows heavy with the smell of sweat and spit and rapture.

"Me neither," she whispers, so quiet I see it in the earnest curve of her mouth more than hear it. So quiet that it might be just for me, that I might be the reason that she, too, has never been anywhere like this before.

Her chin is tilted up. I think she wants me to kiss her.

I think I want to too.

The song ends, and another one starts. Veer shrugs her fingers out of mine and throws her head back, howling or laughing or singing along, I'm not sure which. She dances a few steps back, beckoning me to follow.

"Come on!" she insists, but I'm frozen. I don't know how to do this. I don't know how to be the way she wants me to be.

Her friend in the pink T-shirt is back, wrapping an arm around her shoulders, and Veer holds up one finger and mouths something.

"It's okay," I shout back. It doesn't matter what she said. That's always the right answer.

Veer shrugs and follows her friend, but she's easy enough to track among the other dancers, her white tank top stained blue by the lights. She whips in tighter and tighter circles, wild and feverish, and when the song slows, I watch the ecstatic heave of her shoulders as she catches her breath.

She glances back at me, her gaze like searchlights tracking the night sky. Like I'm a skeleton key, and she's a door that's never been unlocked. Like something I could reach out and grasp, if only I were willing to put my hand out for it.

8

VEER FINDS ME AGAIN WHEN THE SONG CHANGES. WE go back to the kitchen, and she makes me another drink. Mostly tequila, with only a splash of orange juice.

"I can't stay much longer." *Can't* is easier than *shouldn't*.

Veer's face goes expressionless. She thrusts the cup under my nose. "Don't break my heart, now."

It's a cramped kitchen, made even more cramped by the cups scattering every surface like shiny red boils. There's nowhere to retreat.

I take a sip. Taste wet earth with a muted citrus sting. She's still watching me.

I want to see if I can still get it right, if I can prove to her I'm someone worth remembering. I press the pale plastic rim to my lips and hold her gaze and swallow the rest of the drink without pausing to breathe. Her eyes glitter like pools of ink, like twin oil slicks.

"I didn't see you last night," I say, swilling saliva over my tongue to dilute the harsh alcohol aftertaste.

Her crooked canine flashes. "Quiet night. We parked outside a McDonald's and did nothing for, like, three hours."

"Hanging out in a parking lot? What are you, fifteen?"

She snorts. "And who are you, the downtime police?"

"Where would *I* find the time?"

I forgot that I knew how to do this. Or maybe she just makes it easy.

Veer leans back against the counter. "Okay, so you get it. Nap or whatever when you can, right? I mean, I nap. Rodriguez studies." She bends a little to scratch at her hip with her elbow. I'm not sure she even knows she's doing it. "Philosophy."

"No shit."

Her eyebrows spring up, and she makes a face. "I guess that joke only works if you, like, know him. No, he's getting a degree in computer science, gonna ditch me to be a software engineer or something."

"He's smart, huh."

She bristles. "Paramedic cert isn't easy."

"Yeah, I know. I wasn't saying that." She grimaces as if to say, *Sorry, I know.* "But computer science is totally different, right? Lots of math."

She wiggles a finger at me. "Hey, we do lots of math. 0.01 milligrams epinephrine per kilogram, which is 2.2 pounds, so the average anaphylactic ten-year-old takes, uh . . ." The noise of the party swallows the rest of the sentence, and she sticks her tongue out. "Okay, fair, Rodriguez is really smart. So smart I get a little jealous sometimes."

"Because of the math? Or because of the philosophy?"

"That's my partner you're talking shit on." But she's laughing. "And it's not real philosophy. He just says crazy stuff sometimes."

I shift, and an empty beer can topples over on the counter behind me. "Crazy how?"

Her face goes serious for a second, and she drops her voice to mimic Rodriguez's even tone. "Don't waste your life trying to be good, good doesn't exist on a personal level any more than evil does. One person's good deed might inadvertently generate a fuckton of evil in the world. Same deal with one person's evil deed. It's all, like, cosmic. Or karmic." She runs a finger around the rim of the nearest cup. "He gets weird after midnight."

"He sounds like my uncle."

"Does he get weird after midnight too?"

"I don't know. Probably." I remember his jabs about what I should do with my mom. How I'd better quit trying to be a good daughter and get it done. My eyes feel shiny and clouded, and then I realize it's because there are tears there, out of nowhere. I'm suffocating very, very slowly, like gauze is being wadded up in my windpipe one strip at a time.

Veer makes a concerned noise in the back of her throat, and the gauze melts. "Hey. I didn't mean . . ." A twitch in her cheek. "Do you want something to drink?" She glances at the empty orange juice container, then the various glass bottles surrounded by red plastic bodyguards. "Somewhere quiet? Fresh air?"

I swallow. The tears are gone. "I'm fine."

"Okay. Good." She scratches at her waistband again. "You just had a look, for a second."

"An about-to-get-punched-in-the-face look?"

Her high-beam stare fades. "That was such a weird thing to say, wasn't it."

"It's fine." In the background, the music seems to have gotten louder.

Veer shoves off from the counter. We're almost toe-to-toe. "Everything doesn't have to be fine all the time. Come on, want to go out back and punch me in the face for real? Then we'll be even."

I almost start to laugh, but her expression's dead serious. Like she'd let me, if I wanted to.

"I'm good."

She cocks her head to one side. "Kick me in the shins?"

Maybe she's a little drunk too. This time, I do laugh.

"What do you want to do, then?" she asks.

I slide my hand into hers. Her palm is clammy. "We could dance some more."

Maybe I can remember how to do this, after all. Maybe I can still be what she wants.

"Okay," she says as her fingers close over mine. "Cool."

Back into the noise, the shoves, the swirl. Blue-glowed bodies twist together, weight and counterweight. An open hand ricochets out and catches my hair, whistling past my cheek. Veer tugs me closer, her hand twined around my waist, her eyes like endless asphalt roadways. The ground isn't entirely steady under me.

I don't know how to speak this frenzied physical language, so I push closer to Veer instead. Veer, who remembered me. Who sought me out, who froze me out, who is now pressing me against the back of a suede recliner that's been flipped to face the wall. LED afterglow reflects in her eyes like northern lights.

Then it's back. The gauze, the suffocation. Something sharp

edged lodges in my throat. I close my eyes and try to swallow it down, and when I open them again, the glow of the strip-lights has a new, yellow tinge.

I smell the dust of the highway, the slow grind of sand against bone. And blood. Old blood. Sick blood.

"Let's check out the backyard," Veer says abruptly, and she shoves me toward the glitter of a sliding glass door. I don't smell anything now except for sweat and soda and someone's rancid cologne.

There's less yellow grass and more gravel in the back. A couple of people drift in circles, puffing vapes or cigarettes, kicking little sprays of pebbles at each other. One of them waves to Veer, and she waves back. The night air smells like cotton candy flavoring and not enough rain. No blood. No sense of being plunged headfirst into a bucket of water.

"I have something to show you." Veer steers me over to a dusty shed huddled against the side of the house, nighttime draining the color from it until it's just a square-shouldered mass protruding from the stucco. "Think we can get up there?"

She drags a folding chair over, kicks it open on the gravel, then uses it like a step stool to hoist herself onto the shed. She didn't notice anything, in the living room. Maybe it was all in my head.

"Oh shit." Her voice peaks, excited. "Come on."

I scramble up behind her and find Veer drumming on a thin metal ladder attached to the side of the house, obscured by the shadow of the roof.

"Is whoever owns this place okay with us going up there?" I whisper.

Veer makes a face that's enough of an answer. "I'll go first. If the ladder breaks, uh . . ."

"I'll get out of the way."

She chuckles. "What, don't want me on top of you?"

I'm lucky that it's dark and that she's already started to climb, because I don't want to know what my face looks like.

I don't trust the ladder, but it holds together long enough for Veer to scramble onto the roof and for me to follow her. At the top, I fling one leg over the edge and try to roll the rest of the way. It's harder than it looks. Veer tugs on my wrists and I come over a little off-balance, and suddenly we're a tangle of arms and legs, tumbling across the sunbaked surface. My head smacks the corner of a vent, and the world stops spinning.

She has me pinned, her chest on top of mine. Now is when I should kiss her. I want to, desperately, I want to grip her by the back of the neck and pull her into me, I want to—

Devour her, my mind supplies. There, above her eyebrow. Skin scraped off, pink raw promise beneath. My hands move of their own accord, snaking their way into her pomade-slick hair as I press my mouth to the cut and taste salt and dust and triumph.

Veer jerks away. My mouth goes cold.

Then she cups my face and kisses me like a dust storm, like a rattlesnake, with teeth and tongue and no room for breathing. I can barely keep up, not sure where to put my hands, brief moments of panic blotted out by her sheer intensity, like electric sparks in all the places our bodies meet.

When she pulls away, she's breathless, eyes shining.

"Cool," she whispers. She scrunches her nose and pushes off me, adding, "We came all this way, I guess we should check out the view."

Veer kisses me again as we lean into each other on the

edge of the roof. My arm around her shoulders, her fingers playing with my belt loops.

Her nose nudges the base of my ear. “Nice, right?”

The desert is a dark velvet expanse at the edge of the glimmering blanket of city. I can taste the crystalline saltiness of the dry air, the dust that sticks under fingernails and in creases of skin. Wide-open places always call to my family. Places where it’s hard to live, and easy to die. Our hunger feels at home there.

There are more of us out there, I know. Scattered around, or skipping town to town, just like we used to. But my mom says they’re shitty people and we don’t need them, and she’s probably right on at least one of those points. We’re all just scraping by. We don’t have space in our hearts to help one another.

“Yeah.” It’s more than nice. It’s beautiful. “You should probably wash that.”

I gesture at my temple, to show that I mean the cut above her eye.

“Right.” She itches at her hairline. The cut stretches a little wider, glistens a little pinker, and I’m struck breathless by its smell, like scraped knees and pomade. Her gaze is a spotlight again, an interrogation. I watch her mouth a few versions of the question before she asks it.

“You’ve been through some shit too, haven’t you?” She jerks her head, like she’s defending herself from an inaudible retort. “You know what I mean.”

I don’t miss the way she adds *too*, and I can’t stop the sudden, overwhelming sensation that she’s looked right through me and sensed all the things I want to bury.

My pocket buzzes. Veer turns back to the desert as I tug

the phone free, screen screaming to life in my hand. My mom's face, upside down, but still instantly recognizable.

"Sorry," I gasp—to Veer, to the desert, to myself, in preparation for whatever is waiting on the other end of the line—and pick up.

9

"WHERE ARE YOU?" MY MOM DEMANDS. HER VOICE IS tinny and scared.

I glance at Veer and mouth *Sorry* again. "It's okay, Mom. I'm with friends."

"Friends?" Her voice soars, distressed. "What friends? Where did you go?"

I pull the phone away from my ear to glance at the time. 12:17 a.m. "I'll be right there. Are you sleepy? Want to try going back to bed?"

"I'm wide awake." She sharpens the words into an accusation. "I was so worried about you. I won't be able to sleep for hours."

Veer brushes my arm. "I'll go." Before I can stop her, she's swung herself down the ladder and I'm alone on the roof.

"I'll be home soon," I tell my mom. What was I thinking, drinking and dancing and leaving her alone? What kind of a daughter does that? "Put on an episode of TV. I'll be back before it's done, I promise."

"Okay, baby." A raspy breath. I imagine her curled on the couch, knees pulled tight to her chest. "You know I love you."

"I know, Mom. I love you too."

Climbing down, the ladder creaks every time I take a new rung. My mom's the one who banished me. I shouldn't feel bad for doing something other than waiting for her mood to turn. No, that's not fair. She needs me. I scoot my way across the top of the shed, itchy with desperation to get home, to already be home, to have this taken care of and behind me.

As I slip my legs over the side, an impulse drives me to glance back at the roof. All my thoughts catch in my throat.

The house is weeping blood.

Dark stains coalesce in the seams where stucco meets tile. I watch them grow wet and heavy, watch them drip down the walls in swampy blurs. My senses ring with the scent of decay, of sun-scorched earth and maggots so fattened on corpses their bodies burst like tiny, ghastly water balloons.

My marrow quivers with a single phrase, not my own thought but an alien incursion: *I can smell you.*

I slide off the shed and hit the ground hard. My feet are under me and then they aren't, and gravel bites my palms and I'm breathing like I've just run a mile, my sinuses slick with the smell of dead things. I glance back at the house, afraid I'll find it collapsing under the weight of all that gore.

The wall is normal. White stucco, gray shadows. I sniff the air and find only the lingering smells of diet soda and cherry lip balm.

Maybe I'm seeing things as punishment. Maybe I'm losing my mind.

No. Don't. It's just that I'm a little drunk and I haven't been to a party in a long time. Haven't kissed anyone in a long time either.

There's no sign of Veer in the backyard. I don't spot her inside either, and the glamour of the party is gone now. It's all stains on the carpet and the claustrophobia of too many people packed in together. The night is already slipping away, folding me back into the insular world where only my mom and I exist, where I'm never enough and I've lived all this before. It's time to go home.

I order a rideshare, and the driver blasts talk radio all the way back to our apartment.

My mom's asleep in front of the TV. When she opens her eyes, they're bleary and docile, and she doesn't protest as I herd her back into her bedroom and tuck her in. She's so small, I can almost lift her into bed myself.

"Good night, Mom," I whisper. "I love you."

"I knew you'd come back, baby," she mumbles. "You always come back."

I tug her rose-patterned comforter up to her neck and pat her shoulder through it. For a second, I'm tempted to lean down and kiss her forehead, like Uncle Bill did to me, like he used to do to her. But that would be the wrong way around.

"That's right," I tell her. "I'll always come back for you."

Back in the kitchen, I run my tongue across my molars, hoping there might still be something left of Veer there. Need stirs, clawing against my shoulder blades. I'm hungry.

We have five vials left. One vial each per day, so that makes two days till we're out. A little less, if my mom's appetite keeps growing. In the kitchen, I shoot Uncle Bill a text—*Mom told me you called, hope everything's ok. I'll drop by again before work tomorrow*—and focus on the sharp bite of my hunger. I unseal a wipe, drop a fresh needle onto the counter. Which arm was it, last time? Left, probably. I always go left if I'm not thinking. I swab my right forearm, unseal the needle, fill the barrel. Make a fist, hold my breath.

God, it feels good.

There's the usual uncomfortable pinch of metal, the strain of keeping the arm still and getting the angle right, but once the blood's loose inside me it's like sitting down to ice cream after weeks of water and wafers, like jolting awake after an impossibly good night's sleep, no grit in your eyes or sand in your mouth, just euphoria and energy and life, life, *life*. It feels like being me down to the bones, no beast tugging me along like a dog on a chain.

I close my eyes and savor it. The rush fades after a few minutes, dulls back to the same old manageable throb in hours. There was a time, Uncle Bill used to say, chin tucked and eyes watery after a few beers, that creatures like us didn't survive on the bare minimum it took to keep us in human form. People lined up at our feet and offered their arteries, so plentiful no one needed needles. They'd just open their mouths and let their digestive systems waste as much as they wanted.

Stupid stuff. I never liked those stories. Injection's impersonal, safe. After a lifetime of it, it would feel wrong to drink someone's blood. The messiness, the intimacy, hot skin against your lips, the scent of sweat and dirt in your nose, dark hair and lemons and arms looped lazily around your neck, teeth and tongue and iron and—

I sit bolt upright, breathing hard, and get busy getting rid of the needle.

Uncle Bill doesn't text back. Which is fine. He prefers phone calls.

I call him when I'm headed over. He doesn't pick up. My head's a little woolly, and my back is stiff from sleeping like shit. I'd hoped that the morning would shear away some of last night's guilt, but it's still there. I'll make up for it today, somehow.

When I get to Uncle Bill's, all the lights are still off. His truck's still missing. I tell myself the clamminess on the back of my neck is just the hangover, or bad ventilation.

The freezer's still empty. No one's cleaned up the smashed vial in the corner.

I desperately don't want this to be one more thing I have to fix. But there's no one else to do it, and Uncle Bill's family, and we need him. What I want is less important than all of that.

I call him again. Still no answer. I think of the garage walls swollen with blood. The eaves last night, sagging under the weight of it. Maybe I'm being paranoid, but this doesn't feel like Uncle Bill's usual casual disappearance.

I kick open the rock-shaped hide-a-key buried next to the doormat and let myself in. The usual cigarette reek is muted, and the usual burnt coffee smell is missing entirely.

"Uncle Bill?" I call into the lightless hallway. "It's Ellis. You home?"

The hall is piled high with moving boxes. Cardboard flaps clutch at me as I pass. Something wet has spilled or melted in one near the end, turning the stiff brown edge dark and mushy. My heart squeezes as I turn the corner into the kitchen. Maybe I'll find Uncle Bill shuffling to the coffee maker or punching down the toaster button so hard it pops back up rather than sticking. Instead, all I see on the counter is a lone plate and a piece of untoasted bread, an open tub of margarine sweating beside them.

The kitchen's painted shades of brown, with fingerprint-stained white cabinets and stacks of paper plates next to the sink. It smells arid. And something else, something rotten. I push open the fridge and find a steak left marinating, uncovered, on a plate. It's shriveled into a brown mass like a withered organ. The sick mix of Worcestershire sauce and spoiled meat sticks to the inside of my nose. It's not just that, though. A wind-racked rot peeks through the seams of the nasty rotten food stink, a faint smell like a septic wound left weeping.

"Uncle Bill?" I repeat. When the dead quiet stays that way, I dial him again.

A faint buzz that I can delude myself into believing might be coming from my own phone. Then his ringtone trills loud and clear, farther into the house.

I find it in the bathroom, face down and vibrating slowly toward the edge of the counter. The locked screen displays notifications of twelve missed texts, four missed calls, and a bunch of Facebook messages. The battery blinks red: 6 percent.

Uncle Bill's never without his phone. Half the time I see him, he's on the phone with someone. But Uncle Bill's not here, and his phone is, and something is definitely wrong. When I catch my own eye in the bathroom mirror, I look wrong too. Lank and sweaty and spooked. At the angle I'm standing, the corner of the mirror catches a sliver of Uncle Bill's bedroom through the open door.

He keeps a safe under his bed. I only know because he told me, once, with an unusual urgency, that the combination was my birthday. Like it was proof that he cared about me. When

I asked why he was telling me, he grumbled something like "Someone should know, in case something happens to me," and refused to elaborate. Then nothing happened to him, and I mostly forgot about it.

But the safe's not under his bed now. It's lying on its side in the middle of the shitty beige carpet, still locked. Did he leave in a hurry, no time to shove it back into its hiding place?

The house is starting to smell like sand and rot, like chaparral baked brittle by heat, like miles of tiny, dazzling grains hiding the ground beneath, cracked open by thirst.

Inside the safe, I find the deeds to the house and to Uncle Bill's truck, a couple of expired driver's licenses, a yellowed snippet of a *Review-Journal* article about a woman who died in a hiking accident, and a receipt for a handgun. That's just like Uncle Bill, to keep the receipt locked up but the gun itself lying around somewhere. Maybe he took it with him, wherever he's gone. I scrape the contents of the safe out onto the carpet, and a battered Nokia phone I hadn't seen tumbles out after them. Prepaid, probably ten years old and built like a brick, with a strip of masking tape over the back. Scrawled in black Sharpie over it, in Uncle Bill's juvenile handwriting, is a note: *Emergencies only!!!* I jam my thumb into the little on button, but the battery's dead.

I plug Uncle Bill's iPhone into the charger next to his bed and shove the Nokia into my pocket as something surprisingly close to a sob rises in my throat. I don't know where Uncle Bill's gone, I don't know why, I don't know when—if—he's coming back. And I don't know what to do.

It's just the hangover, I promise myself, and the eeriness of the empty house. It's just because we rely on him, and he keeps letting me down.

Outside, a dog yips and whines. Right. There's a world outside, sun and road and patients waiting. I'd better get to work.

The dog barks, louder this time. Louder than is reasonable, given I'm inside the house. I breathe in, and the smell of carrion grips me by the throat. Then comes the wind.

Desert winds always sweep through Las Vegas with the changing of the seasons, whipping sand into your eyes and swaying long-haul trucks on Highway 95. But this wind smells wrong, like sun-bleached skulls and withered limbs, like biting into rotting fruit.

I don't want to find out, but I have to.

Someone's smashed the window of Uncle Bill's office. Glass like grains of rice scatters the desk. Beneath it, half-soaked into the tufted carpet, is a spreading pool of liquid about the size of a pair of footprints. From the smell, I know it's blood, but there's something wrong with it. Not red and drying, but viscous and oil colored and stinking of decay.

It doesn't smell like Uncle Bill. I don't know whether or not to be relieved by that.

A noise like static in my ears. At first I think it's the computer—who breaks into a house only to leave the computer and the safe?—but then I realize it's my fear, transmuted into a buzzing plea to be anywhere but here.

When I try to back out of the room, my sneaker meets the computer tower nestled under the desk. The monitor screams to life in a blaze of white light. He doesn't have a password, so when the screen fades into a perceptible image, it's his inbox.

The wind spits through the broken window, whipping my hair into my eyes. There's nothing from the past week in his inbox. The older stuff is all automated bill pay reminders, a few months-old personal emails, and something from an email group called *map-western-us* that is either blank or won't load. There's nothing recent in his sent mail either.

I find something in his drafts.

Hey man, it reads. There's no subject line, and no address in the "To" field. *I couldn't get you on the phone. I know this sounds crazy, but*

That's as far as he got. But there are notes underneath, things he wanted to say but hadn't decided on the right words for. The first one reads, *Flayed man . . . what do they call them here?*

Has my mom been tormenting Uncle Bill with this flayed man stuff too?

The other notes don't give me any answers:

Telepathic?? Waking dreams?

MR and RV both 2017, Mt Charleston disappearances (unconfirmed)

The wind picks up even more, scraping cold fingers over my neck as I copy what he's written into my phone. I'll search it later, see if it means anything.

"Flayed men are just a story, right?" I asked Uncle Bill once, trying to make it sound like I didn't care, like I already knew the answer. Like my mom's threats of calling him didn't work on me anymore.

He swirled the coffee around in his mug, staring at it like it was the most exciting thing in the world. "Sure, Ellie. They're just a story. Same way that when politicians make promises, it's just a story. Or in court, when they're trying to convince the jury."

"Okay," I pressed, "but he's not really hunting us, is he? He's not actually real?"

"What I was trying to say was," he continued, not really

answering my question, "the whole world is propped up by stories, and some of them are exaggerations or just plain lies, but some . . ." He paused for a long time, swilling coffee around his mouth. "I mean, look at us."

I shut down the computer and take out the trash, and when I'm standing on the curb, I can almost convince myself not to be afraid.

I drive too fast all the way to work, with the GPS on at top volume even though I don't need it, the Nokia plugged into my car charger and the windows down to keep my senses full of the smell of air and sand. To keep my mind off Uncle Bill and what I'm going to do next.

I know what I want to do next. I want to shut my eyes and wake up in my bed, with Uncle Bill calling me. I want to box up the terror that started to press in on me back at the house and put it away and never have to look at it again. I want none of this to be real. Maybe the next best thing is pretending that it isn't.

Except I can't do that, because we need blood.

That doesn't mean I know what to do. The loneliness is the worst part. I can't ask my mom, and no one else will understand.

Maybe the knife-sharp creature inside me will have an answer. It's the worst of me, but it's also the only part of me that doesn't know how to lie. I wait until I hit an arterial, where I can keep driving without paying too much attention, and part my lungs and reach my awareness toward the iron bars.

"What would you do?" I ask it.

The answer comes not as a word but as an impulse—a lunge forward, legs outstretched, ears pinned back.

Run.

The windshield blurs into a screen of pure red, like I've run through a car wash, only it's not water, it's blood. The rancid smell of carrion gags me. I hit the brakes and someone honks, very far away, as a message worms its way into my mind again, just like it did at the party.

Not long now.

"Turn left," the GPS burbles in her clipped, inhuman voice. I snap back to myself just in time to catch a middle finger from the driver passing me. My windshield is clear.

I dig my nails into the steering wheel and turn. What else can I do? But that single syllable, *run*, echoes in my ears like a drumbeat until I pull into the hospital parking lot.

10

BY THE TIME I PULL INTO THE HOSPITAL PARKING LOT, Uncle Bill's burner phone has enough of a charge to turn on. It only has one number saved: a northern Nevada area code under the contact name Brian. I try calling, but he doesn't answer. I tuck it into my pocket, just in case.

I don't even think about Veer until she finds me in the break room.

She and Rodriguez roll in along with another pair—the loud, bossy one is Temple, I think, and the stone-faced one is Ying—as I'm finishing my lunch break. Coffee and crackers. Eleven at night isn't really lunchtime anyway.

"We picked up Oscar again," Temple drawls, slamming her way through the cabinets in search of K-Cups. "Come on, how hard is it not to smoke when you're already on oxygen?"

Ying grunts.

"He's lonely," Rodriguez says in his soft, measured tone. "People do messed-up things, sometimes, when they get old and don't have anyone left to care."

"We're not babysitters," Temple grumbles, but quieter.

I smell Veer's distinctive mix of sweat and skin and hair gel, but she doesn't say anything. Not to them, or to me. The back of my neck itches.

Temple scrapes one of the chairs toward herself. "Is this seat taken?"

She sits before I answer, legs splayed wide. She smells like drive-through hash browns and whitening strips. EMTs and medics see a lot, not just the body stuff but having to come to people wherever they are, in whatever state they're in. Sometimes it shrinks them down, makes them melancholy and reflective like Rodriguez or expressionless and guarded like Ying. Sometimes it makes them like Temple, confident that she's seen the worst of life already. Sometimes it makes them like Veer, quick to anger and quicker to remorse. Is that what she meant by having been through some shit?

"It's yours," I say. I don't have it in me to be around people right now. "I was just finishing up."

I toss my coffee and head for the door, but a hand on my arm stops me.

"Hey," Veer says. "I'll walk with you."

Temple tips back in her chair. "Hands to yourself, Zawadski."

"Fuck off," Veer calls, half joking, as the door slams behind us. She grimaces. "Sorry."

Her hand falls away from my arm. I want to catch it and bring it back, but we're at work and it's not like that. She's stuck a round Band-Aid over the scrape on her eyebrow. I like how her lips turn up at the corners. I want her to kiss me again.

Instead, she asks, "Back to triage?"

I'd wanted to swing by the fifth-floor break room, where the phlebotomists swap blood-draw horror stories, to find out what I could about the hospital's management of blood samples. Maybe get closer to a solution that doesn't rely on faith that Uncle Bill will turn up overnight, or that the mysterious Brian will call me back. But I can't tell Veer any of that, so instead I tell her, "Yeah."

"Cool."

A nurse in Sleeping Beauty scrubs passes us, clacking hot-pink nails on her clipboard. Veer's sneakers squeak on the tile. I wish I knew what to say to bring back whatever intimacy we had last night. But it's gone now, maybe proof that it was never real to begin with. She's sobered up, and this is the part where she's nice enough to apologize for everything.

Abruptly, she stops.

"Last night was all right, yeah?" She asks it like a challenge.

"Yeah."

"So, like. Want to do it again?"

I can't help a laugh. "Almost start a fight and then go to a party and then I run out on you because my family's a mess?"

Her eyebrows punch up as if to say, *Oh right, that.* "Okay, so not exactly the same thing. But would you, like, want to go for a drink or something? Not tomorrow, I'm going up to Reno, but maybe next week if we both have a night off?"

It's been a while since someone's asked me out, even longer since I've wanted to say yes. I want to get to know her. I want to ask her what she meant about her darkness. I want to see her in that cutoff tank top again.

"That sounds nice," I say, and the eager flash in her eyes is like a knife in my back, "but I can't. You know, the family stuff."

She wouldn't get it. She didn't even ask if my mom's okay.

I brace for an accusation, the kind my mom deploys when

I'm too wrapped up in myself to play along. Veer only backs away, shrugs, doesn't quite meet my eyes.

"No problem," she says. "It's cool. Uh, you have my number."

My pocket vibrates. I whip out my phone, ready for my mom's face to blare accusingly from the screen, but it's blank. The call's coming from my other pocket. The one with Uncle Bill's burner phone in it.

The break room door whines shut. Veer's gone. I pull the silver Nokia free and it buzzes across my palm, green-and-black screen blinking furiously.

Incoming Call: Brian.

I hit the green button and for a second, it's just dead air and I'm cold with panic. Then—

"Hello?" His voice is gruff and wary, fuzzy around the edges from the ancient phone and bad reception.

"Hi," I answer, breathless. "Is this Brian?"

"Who's this?"

Of course. He was expecting Uncle Bill. "My name's Ellis. I'm Bill Karsten's niece. I—"

"How'd you get this phone?"

My feet are taking me somewhere quiet. Not the break room, a bathroom maybe, or an empty patient room. I can't have this conversation out in the open, but I also can't ask him to call back later and risk never hearing from him again.

"I found it." I push past more nurses with more clipboards, past patients pacing the halls. "Have you seen him lately? He hasn't been home and I haven't heard from him in a couple days, and I found this old phone with your number for emergencies and I just need—"

I bite it off at the last second. I don't know if he's one of us.

"Bill's niece." He chews on each word. "His sister's kid?"

"Yeah." I swing into a patient room and shut the door behind me. Wind shrieks in the background of the call, filling in the space where Brian's quiet.

"So you're family."

It's the same roundabout language Uncle Bill uses: Hunger makes family of all of us, biological or otherwise. I hate this dance, the euphemisms. If I have to beg, I'd rather do it honestly, knees ground into the dirt, the ticking clock of my body exposed for the vultures.

But I don't get to choose how I do it. I've lost control. Of this, of my mom, of my thoughts that keep swirling back to the disappointment in Veer's eyes as she walked away.

"Yeah," I say. "Family."

"Well." He pops the last syllable, adding a "p" where there isn't one. "I haven't heard from him. And you shouldn't go through his stuff. Never know what you might find." There's a note of warning to that last bit.

"I didn't—" I stop myself, try to refocus. "I don't know when he'll be back, and his freezer's empty."

I thought Brian might know what that means. But his "Okay" tells me he doesn't.

"Blood," I say, voice hushed, tasting salt and resentment because now that I'm saying it out loud to this stranger, I understand why Uncle Bill keeps the word in the crook of his elbow but not on his tongue. Saying it out loud feels shameful, no matter how many times you smell it, no matter how many times you thrust it into your veins. "We're running low, and if he doesn't come back soon . . ."

"How low?"

I think of the vials smashed across our floor, of my mom's blackened tongue, of the nearly full sharps container. "A couple days."

He swears. The wind howls in the background, staticky and muffled. I find myself staring out of the hospital room window into the concrete wall outside. *No Parking*, it demands in blocky white letters. They'll be wondering where I am at the triage desk.

Brian coughs. "You got a car?"

"Yeah."

"Come up this week. I'll text you the coordinates."

Relief floods my lungs. He's willing to help. Ten, twenty, a hundred small failures brought me here, but I've staved off adding one more.

"Where—" I start, but he's already hung up.

I stand there, looking out the window into a concrete void, and without warning all my limbs turn to lead weights. I slide into the room's single pea-colored vinyl chair and wrap my arms around myself.

"This is good," I whisper. "It's going to be okay."

It's the kind of thing I say to my mom when she's upset. Phrases that don't really mean anything, but I've been saying them so long that I'm not sure I know how to do anything else.

I breathe in, parse the smells of floor polish and Windex, of papery hospital gowns and strangers' fingerprints left on the TV remote. The hospital air's familiar funk of body fluids and exhaustion, of people stretched thin and wrung out. It really is going to be okay. I've bought us time, and a few more days of hoping that Uncle Bill comes back.

If he doesn't, it proves all my mom's fears right, the ones whispering that everyone leaves her, that I'm the only one who won't, and not even because I don't want to, but because I owe her. Will I have to be the one to break it to her that he's gone for good?

The Nokia buzzes, reminding me it's still in my hand. Brian's texted coordinates. I plug them into my phone, find he's way out in the northern Nevada desert. For a second, I taste exhaust and shadow and tumbleweed.

I'll text when I'm on the way, I reply.

Then, belatedly, *Thank you.*

The phone buzzes. *You're welcome. Bill is a good guy. I'm sure he'll be back soon.*

That, too, feels like a lie.

11

AFTER WORK, IN THE SECRECY OF MY BEDROOM, I SIT cross-legged on the comforter and dial the customer service number for the UNLV medical center. It's the only way I can think of to reach Uncle Bill's work. Maybe he called in sick. Maybe they know something.

"For English, please press 1," the automated voice croons. I press 1.

I've slept in the same twin bed for sixteen years. Blue sheets, blue pillows, blue paisley bedspread, swirls of light blue and dark blue and somewhere-in-the-middle blue the same color as the crisscross of blue veins on the backs of my hands. I start to wonder what Veer would think of it, then cut that thought off before it's finished. It doesn't matter. It's not a good idea.

"To help us connect you, please select from the following menu items," the voice chirps. "If this is an emergency, please hang up and call 911."

It's not that kind of emergency. Can I delude myself into

believing it's not an emergency at all? By the time I've tried, and failed, and tried and failed again, the menu has looped back to the beginning.

"To schedule an appointment, please press 1" finally gives way to "For all other questions, please press 0." I punch my thumb down on the 0 on my phone screen.

A second of silence. Then, "Hi, you've reached the University of Nevada, Las Vegas, Wellness Center. Please leave a message, and we will return your call as soon as we can."

I open my mouth to leave a message, then hang up instead. What if I'm overreacting? I can't fuck up Uncle Bill's job. He needs it. *We* need it. The wind draws whispering fingers over my window, and, suddenly, I want to cry.

Uncle Bill's an asshole, always has been, unreliable and sullen and quick with passive aggression disguised as straight talk. But with my mom's memory fraying, he's also the person who remembers me best in the world. And I'd rather worry about him than the empty freezer, or my weird visions, or my mom's fantasies of the flayed man.

"Families like ours used to live where the earth was hungriest" was how my mom began the story of the flayed man, or at least, the version I remember best. She told it often enough when I was four and five, syringe in my hand, painfully trial-and-erroring my way into my own veins, but she wasn't always consistent in her retellings. "Marshes, swamps, border places where solid ground stops being so solid anymore. He was a priest, or our version of one. He found the children lost in the bogs, the trapped ones, the drowned ones, and brought them back to feed his family."

This was a noble act, her voice said. He was a good man, once. But it only takes one mistake to doom you forever.

"Eventually, people stopped venturing into the swamp. And his family began to starve. Until one day, he came upon a woman trapped in quicksand. Blinded by hunger, he didn't hesitate. He devoured her. And then, only when he had licked his jaws clean of the last drop of her blood, did he realize: it was his own daughter."

She said it with a smile. It's so easy for the universe to turn on us.

"For what he'd done, the flayed god cursed him to wander the swamps forever, unable to return to his human form. Killing and killing, eating and eating, and still he's always starving. He can hear your innermost thoughts, and if you're naughty, if you're ungrateful, he'll be drawn to you. No matter how fast you run, he'll find you. And then, well. He likes the taste of hearts best."

An ancient priest shrouded in layers of torn flesh, rib cage cracked apart, joints ground down and bent back, every nerve exposed and screaming to feed. That's what we'd become too, without blood to keep us under control. That's why it's up to me to do whatever it takes to make sure my mom's hunger is taken care of, and her with it.

But not yet. Not yet.

I barely realize what I'm doing until the Nokia is in my hand. The T9 keypad makes typing slow and frustrating.

Did uncle Bill ever tell you about this urban legend called the flayed man?

Painstakingly, I add more.

idk if you have it here, it might be a local thing where my grandma is from. I found an email he started about it and thought he might have been writing to you. Btw I'll drive up tomorrow.

As soon as the phone chimes to indicate the text is sent, I want to take it back. It's a weird question, and Brian was barely friendly on the phone. What if this is all it takes to change his mind about helping us?

I can't bring myself to let the Nokia out of my sight as I microwave a dinner of frozen rice and vegetables. The tiny screen stays dark. I wash my face and brush my teeth, and when I'm done, I'm tempted to start all over again. Scrub my skin clearer, my teeth shinier. I pick at an imaginary blemish near my eyebrow.

When your body heals the way ours do, it's easy to use it to punish yourself. I used to be worse: picking at my skin, chewing away hangnails. Digging the opaque ridge of my thumbnail into my forearm, where I could see veins drawing their blue tracks. I wanted to tear my flesh away until I could pull my arteries free of their predestined routes, until I could snap them between my molars. Then I'd really have something to be afraid of.

A sensation like a sharp pinch, and I look up to see that I've scraped the top layer of skin off where I was poking at the non-blemish. It's red and raw now, a self-fulfilling prophecy.

I wash my face again. No flecks of pink on the white towel. It's already healed. The Nokia remains blank faced on the counter.

I need to take my mind off waiting for Brian to reply.

I stretch my thoughts back to Uncle Bill's email draft. The initials and dates are probably a dead end with no context, but the bit about disappearances might lead somewhere.

I type *Mt Charleston disappearances (unconfirmed)*, just how Uncle Bill wrote it, into Google and hold my breath.

A few local news articles pop up, along with a website

detailing cold cases and an *Unsolved Mysteries* Reddit post. Avalanche a few years ago, missing family on a camping trip, mystery car abandoned near a trailhead. Nothing specific enough to let me be sure of what I'm looking for.

I scroll until my back starts to ache. Then I have another idea. I dig through my work bag until I find the papers I pulled from Uncle Bill's safe.

A newspaper cutting, the one about the woman who died in a hiking accident, surfaces with a rustle of old paper and the smell of burnt coffee. There's a faint brownish ring in the upper corner, where Uncle Bill must have set his coffee mug.

A little over a year ago, Martina Revelle, forty-six, went out for the day and never came back. Her neighbor saw her drive off, said she had no idea where Martina was going but that she often went on long solo hikes. The first day she didn't come back, the neighbor figured she was camping. She called the cops on the second day. There are no friends quoted, and no family, but that could mean anything. Maybe Martina Revelle was just a normal person who no one liked.

Except Uncle Bill cut out an article about her disappearance and locked it in his safe. That's not normal.

I pull out my laptop and Google her. "Martina Revelle" returns the online version of the *Review-Journal* article, and the same info rehashed by the other local news sites. A follow-up article says her car was found abandoned near Corn Creek, doors flung open, overrun by wildlife. I keep scrolling, keep clicking through the pages until they devolve into forum threads and those spam sites that copy articles but change every few words until they're nonsense.

One of the Reddit threads catches my eye. It's titled "Weird True Crime Stories—Las Vegas," which seems kind of flippant, but it's a true crime subreddit and I don't really get that stuff. Half of a comment has caught in the Google search, a mention of Martina's name and a long paragraph that cuts off midway through, so I open it up and scroll down until I find the full thing.

> This happened near the end of my senior year and my friends and I became kind of obsessed with it. We placed bets about whether they'd find her body before graduation. Sorry, morbid.
>
> We heard from my friend's older brother that there were all these strange details that were never reported online. I don't think it was because of her family's wishes, it seemed like she didn't have any family around, but if it was, sorry and no disrespect. Let's be real though, we all know LVMPD. Way more likely it's a cover-up lol.
>
> Ok so, a couple days before she disappeared, Martina basically had a psychotic break. According to this, she went from a reliable CVS cashier and all around pretty regular lady to completely paranoid, not sleeping, screaming at anyone who knocked on the door or came near her. Someone else in her building posted on Facebook that they heard sounds of crying and glass breaking.

I try both links, one a blog and one a Facebook link, but both return an error. No one sharing information about

Martina at the time cares enough now to still keep it public. The post continues:

> When they found her car, there was blood all over the driver's seat. But here's the weird thing: it wasn't her blood. Our guess was, if it was a criminal or a murderer the police would have said so, so they must not have known whose it was.
>
> I kinda drifted away from those friends tbh, but I still think about Martina sometimes. She was born the same year as my mom. It's sad to think that if she hasn't turned up by now, she probably never will.

I try to swallow, but the movement gets stuck somewhere in my throat. Then I thumb back through my Notes app.

MR and RV both 2017

Martina Revelle disappeared from northern Las Vegas in the spring of 2017. She's MR. Why keep tabs on her, though?

Maybe she was Uncle Bill's girlfriend. Not like I know much about his dating life.

Or maybe she was one of us.

The Reddit post is four months old, but when I click through to the writer's profile, they're still active on various true crime subreddits. God, there are a lot of unsolved murders in Vegas. Still, that means there's a chance they'll respond to a message.

Uncle Bill was looking into these disappearances, so if I can learn more about Martina and figure out who RV is, I might be able to retrace his steps. It's better than doing nothing and hoping he comes back.

I set up a profile and start typing. *Hi there. I'm interested in Martina Revelle too. I saw her car was found near Corn Creek, but do you know exactly where?*

I hit send and stretch into bed, phone on the pillow next to me, unable to close my eyes. I don't realize I've fallen asleep until I'm jerked awake again by a demanding whistle. Brian's texted back.

See you tomorrow.

I haven't ruined anything. Not yet, at least.

I don't bother to get up, just shove the Nokia under my pillow and turn over to get as much rest as the day will still allow me. Only when I'm already halfway there, my body grown numb and distant with sleep, do I wonder if there's a reason he didn't answer my question.

12

JOANNE LIVES IN THE APARTMENT DIRECTLY ABOVE ours. I hear her sometimes, when I'm not at work, shuffling back and forth in the eye-watering hours of the morning. I don't think she sleeps much. I have to knock four times before she unlocks the door, and then it's only a crack, chain pulled tight, her face wedged out of the slice of darkness beyond.

"Oh," she says. She smells like too much skin and not enough blood. "Hi, honey."

She shuts the door again to unlatch the chain and swings it all the way open. Stale, frigid air rushes free. I fight the urge to cross my arms.

"Hey, Joanne." I hope my smile spans both gratitude and desperation. "Can I ask you a favor?"

"Sure, sure." She inches forward to lean against the doorframe, her pupils dilating as the sun hits them. Her pity stinks of iron and bile. "How's your mom?"

"She's okay." Then I remember that the last time Joanne

saw her, she was brandishing a wooden spoon and spitting violent fury. "Better than when you came by."

I think Joanne can tell it's a lie, because the pity grows so strong I can almost taste it. Brussels sprouts and boiled cabbage. Plastic bags and cellophane wrap. Behind her, the TV sings a fast-food jingle, garbled by the buzz of the air conditioner.

"That's good." Her sympathy makes me feel like a puppet with its strings cut. "What can I do for you?"

I explain that I have to go out of town tomorrow. "Family thing," I say, and she nods, because Mom's told her stories about Uncle Bill, or at least cursed his name in front of her enough times that she's familiar—and could she pop in tomorrow morning if it's not too much trouble, just to make sure my mom's okay and not too confused about where I've gone, and to make sure she gets her medicine.

"Two kinds of pills," I tell her. "I'll send you a picture of the bottles. One of each pill, you can just remind her and make sure she doesn't double up. She also has a liquid medication."

This is the part that scares me.

"I'll mix it before I leave. It's really important that she drinks the whole thing. She might not want to, but she has to take it every day. It's for her heart."

Another lie, but her heart is something Joanne will understand.

"Of course," Joanne says. "I'll make sure she drinks it."

Behind her, *Days of Our Lives* lights up the TV. She glances over her shoulder, too polite to say she's eager to get back to it but making it obvious enough to hope I'll get the hint.

"Thanks." She starts to shut the door, but at the last second,

I add, "I'll mix it before she goes. The medicine. I'll text you a photo of the cup before I leave too."

"No problem. It's always a pleasure to help with your mom."

There. Now we're both lying.

"Thanks, Joanne. Take care. I'll text you."

The door's already mostly shut, but I catch her "Hope your uncle's doing well" before the scrape of the lock and the noise of the TV turned up.

Hope your uncle's doing well. I think of the way he never finished that email, like he was in too much of a hurry to get—where? Wherever Martina went, leaving behind a car filled with blood that wasn't hers?

I take the turn of the stairwell too tight, and the hem of my sweatshirt catches on the railing. The stairwell windows are coated in dust the color of dead leaves, and the light that filters through is browner and weaker every time I pass. Winds are picking up. We've had a lot of asthma attacks in the ED lately.

I haven't told my mom yet, not about Brian or what happened at Uncle Bill's house or the fact that it means I have to leave her. It's only a day and a half. If I leave now, I'll get to Reno by dinnertime. Sleep in the car, do the final couple hours in the morning, turn around and drive straight back. I took today and tomorrow off work, so I won't even have to head to the hospital right after I get home.

But for my mom, a day isn't always a day. Sometimes it's an eternity. Sometimes the length of time doesn't matter, because no matter how short it is, it still means I'm leaving her.

My toe catches on the welcome mat, and I kick it back into place with too much force. I'm ready for tears, I tell myself. I'm ready for screaming. I will meet them stone faced because this is what I need to do, for her, for us. And because she'll forget.

I find my mom in the living room, legs tucked underneath her like a schoolgirl on portrait day. She's inspecting the backs of her hands, twisting them this way and that like she can't quite understand what she's seeing.

"My hands." She doesn't look up. "They're not right."

When I was young, my mom was so proud of her pale, smooth, wrinkle-free hands, prouder of them even than her equally wrinkle-free face. The cloying scent of her hand cream always smelled to me like love, and like an unpaid debt. But I'm not young anymore, and her hands, while still slender and fine boned, are traced with wrinkles and spots of discoloration.

I take a deep breath. "Mom, I have to go up to Reno."

She doesn't respond. Just keeps staring at her hands. She pulls on the cuticle of the ring finger, watching the skin whiten and stretch.

"Mom, I talked to a friend of Uncle Bill's, and he's going to help us out. To replace the vials you . . . never mind. Anyway, he's up north, so I'm going to have to—"

"They don't look like my hands." She sounds on the verge of tears. "Am I losing my mind?"

Yes, the spiteful thing that lurks beneath my tongue tempts me to say. Yes, yes, and it's worse every day. Instead, I fold myself at her feet and wrap her betraying hands in mine.

"You're not losing your mind," I assure her. "You're a little confused, that's all. Now, listen, I have to leave for a day, like I said, just to go see Uncle Bill's friend, but I'll be back tomorrow night. And I'm only a phone call away. Okay?"

"Oh." She settles disconsolately into her chair, staring dead eyed into the black glass of the turned-off TV. "Okay."

No tears. No screaming.

"You'll be fine," I murmur, squeezing her hands in mine, trying to soothe myself almost as much as I'm trying to soothe her.

"I'll be fine," she repeats miserably.

My legs protest as I get up, my arms growing sluggish as I sling my duffel bag over one shoulder. It isn't fair to keep all these secrets from her. Uncle Bill is her brother, she should know if he's missing.

I'll tell her soon. When I get back.

I'm nervous, too, about leaving her with Joanne. Joanne isn't family. She can't be trusted to care about my mom like I do.

"Hey, Mom?" I'm not sure what brings it into my mind. "You haven't seen the flayed man recently, have you?"

The chair squeaks. She twists and untwists her ankles. I want her to reassure me that no one strange has been around, imaginary creature or otherwise.

"Don't talk about him," she spits. "It's bad luck."

Her hands, too, start to twist and untwist. I should leave it be. But delusions are rooted in reality. If someone's been trying to get into the apartment, I can't leave town. Joanne can't keep her safe like I can.

"So you have seen him?" I ask, trying to make it sound gentle.

She rockets upright, no longer docile. "Of course I've seen him. He's cutting pieces out of me. He's making me like this. Don't talk about him!"

"Mom, he's not—" Don't say it. So I fell for her mind

games again, worrying about someone spying on her when she's really only after someone to blame.

"He is!" she shrieks. Her face is red with fear and fury. "He knows things, Ellis. He knows about you!"

I think of the other night, of kissing Veer as the desert watched. "What does he know about me?"

"He knows that you're doing this." She gestures to the Post-its that I've already needed to replace around the room. *Keep the TV volume below 10. Check if the dishes are dirty before you put them away.* "You need me to be weak, you need me to need you. You won't let me get better! You won't let me do things on my own!"

"Nobody is doing anything to you." She's confused and inventing explanations for the things that scare her. But it still hurts, like a loose tooth torn out. "You're sick, okay, Mom? It started about two and a half years ago, and it's been getting worse, and it's not me. I'm not doing anything to you, I'm doing it *for* you. I love you. Remember? I'm doing this because someone has to. Who the fuck else is going to? Uncle Bill?" My voice hitches. Don't cry. Not now. "And, you know what? It's a lot, and sometimes I don't know how to help you, so can you please just let me go up north and fix things. When I get back, we can sit down and read your medical records, we can make a plan if you want to go out more, whatever you want. Just, please, Mom. Please."

I'm breathless, my mouth sour. I don't even know what I'm begging for. I just want her to understand.

"Fuck you, Ellis," she spits. Her eyes are bright and for a second, there's a flash of the real her, the one whose mind is sharp and tongue is sharper. I almost feel relief.

Then the words register.

"Fuck you," she repeats, and my mom never swears at me, never, or she never has but now she does. "I raised you to be respectful, and I was so patient even when you talked back, even when you were a real brat. And you were a real brat. You know that?"

My breath clogs my throat. I know, I know, I know. The fact that it still makes me angry, that it turns me against her just like she always claimed, is proof that it's true.

"You're a grown-up now, and you think it's okay to tell your mom she's helpless and then waltz out the door for days on end? You really think I'll believe you're off on some pure-hearted errand? You're just like me. You'll do whatever you want."

She, too, is best at getting angry out of nowhere. Maybe that's where I learned it.

"And by the way, I feel fine. Maybe there's something wrong with you. Ever considered that? Maybe you're the problem. Maybe you're putting this all on me, like, like, like . . . you know what I mean. You spent all that time studying mental disorders. Don't you think you might have a mental disorder? You're obsessed with me, with controlling me. You never let me do anything, you resent me for, for, for . . ." She trails off, breathing hard.

"Mom," I try. "Mom, I don't. Please. I'm sorry."

"Oh, you will be sorry." Malice in her eyes. Then, abruptly, it fades, and her face goes slack and devastated.

"Ellis?" Her expression is pitiful. Confused. "Baby, are you mad at me?"

"No. No, of course not."

She squints at me. "Yes, you are. I can tell. You're always so mad at me. Why can't you tell me what I'm doing wrong?

Why do you have to punish me?" She sniffs. "I tried so hard, ever since you were a baby, and you always pushed me away. I know I wasn't always a good mom, but I was doing my best. I just wanted the best for you."

"I know." Please, Mom. I know.

"You know." Her tone turns flat, contemptuous. "You know, you know. You always know best." She wipes her nose on the back of her hand, and it comes away smudged with pink lipstick. "Why do you hate me? Just tell me, and you can go. Leave, do whatever you want. Just tell me. Please, baby. I need to know."

Even sick, she still knows how to manipulate me. She's known my soft parts since she held me as a baby, and she's kept them within reach ever since, so she can poke at them to remind me of what I owe her. It would be too simple to say that the last few years have loosened her tongue and sharpened her edges. Wasn't she always like this?

The truth is, I don't remember anymore.

"I don't hate you." I sound so tired. I sound like a liar. "How about you sit down? I'll make you a cup of tea. You can watch something on TV?"

She hesitates a second, considering. "Okay. Tea, please."

I want to be alone. I want to nurse my aches and my anger, and I can't do that here, not with her around. At least I've managed to defuse things. I ease my bag to the ground and turn the dial on the stove, but it clicks impotently. I try again. Off. On. Off. The burner roars to life, flames leaping up to lick my fingers.

As I jerk my hand back, my mom says, "Ellis?"

"Yes?" And I turn around just in time to catch the sneaky, spiteful gleam at the edge of her expression.

"I don't want you to leave."

Her slippers shuffle on linoleum, and then she's through the door, slamming it behind her. I fumble with the stove, leap for the doorknob, dash after her. A pause on the landing, the slam of the back stairs, and I catch her rounding the stairwell, almost hopping every few steps as if one of her legs has got pins and needles.

"Mom!" I shout. "Where are you going?"

She glances at me over her shoulder, eyes sparkling in defiance, before swinging the stairwell door open and rushing into the parking lot. I nearly trip over my own feet trying to sprint down the stairs two at a time after her. I catch the door on the backswing and hurtle into the dust and dazzle of the outside world. For a second, everything is tinted a sickly yellow, a vomitous film spread over the inside of my eyelids, and my senses fill with the scent of disease, of dried-out flesh and decaying roots.

Then all of that is gone, and I hear only my mom's familiar shout of triumph and a waterfall crash of breaking glass.

13

WHEN I'VE BLINKED THROUGH THE DAYTIME BRIGHTNESS, I see my mom swaying there, a chunk of cement in her hand—where did she get that from?—and a smug look on her face. My car windshield is a kaleidoscope of spiderweb cracks.

"This," I say. My face is hot. My whole body's hot. "This is why I hate you. Because I'll never be good enough for you, and you think that means you don't ever have to listen to me." Am I shouting? My mouth is moving on its own. "And you know what? You need me more than I need you! Can't you get that? You need me! So why can't you just fucking listen?"

She falters. Is it because I rarely see her outside, in the sunlight, that I haven't noticed how old she looks? My legs are shaking. I reach for her, but I can't get the right words out and suddenly I'm afraid of making it worse, of saying something unforgivable. Maybe I already have.

"Ellis?" She's near tears again. "Are you okay?"

No, Mom, I'm not okay. I haven't been okay for a long time, maybe ever. I was born with a prison in my heart, but you made a prison of my life. Or maybe I made it, because you built the iron bars, but I was the one who stepped inside and handed you the key.

"Of course I'm okay," I reassure her. My eyelashes are wet. I'm not supposed to be crying. "Go upstairs. I'll be there in a few minutes."

She does it. Gentle, obedient, leaning heavily on the railing as she hoists herself up, stair by stair. I scrub my eyes with my fists until the tears are erased.

There's something rotting me from the inside. Maybe that's all I am, really, the rot, and the rest of me is just my mom's imagination.

It doesn't matter. I still have to take care of her, which means I have to stop feeling sorry for myself and start figuring out how I'm going to make it to northern Nevada now that she's busted my car. I'll go for a walk, get my head together.

Our neighborhood is a suburban facade starting to show its cracks. Sprawling apartment buildings and beat-up single-family homes with trucks in the driveways. Patchy grass. No neighborhood watch signs. I get two blocks, then perch on the edge of someone's cinder block planter and call the first mechanic that pops up when I search.

"Sure," he says. "Six hundred bucks."

"Okay." Like I have that kind of money on hand. "Can you have it done by tomorrow?"

His laugh is a hoarse bark. Then he realizes I'm serious. "Sorry, ma'am, but it'll take a few days to get the replacement windshield in. You'll have to call around and find some place that already has one."

I thank him and hang up. The sun's making my shoulders

itch. I call three more places, and they all quote me about the same price and the same timeline.

I can't wait for a replacement windshield. Brian's expecting me, and there isn't enough blood left in the freezer for me to reschedule.

I try rental car places next. But it's spring break and tourists are coming and going with advance reservations, and no one seems quite sure they'll have a car for me that's not a monster truck like Uncle Bill's and as expensive to rent for a few days as my windshield will be to replace. Like I can cover the expense of both. Like I can even cover the expense of one, really, on top of bills and food and my mom's medications.

But what other choice do I have? I tell the rental car place I'll be there in an hour, and I call the mechanic to say I'll drop the car off as soon as I can.

"Stay safe," the mechanic says. "If you have AAA, you know, you can get a free tow."

That gives me an idea. Uncle Bill's truck. I dial 311. When I wipe my free hand on the edge of my shorts, the skin of my thigh goes white and chalky where I press it.

"Hello," I say once I get past three levels of automated menu, "have you towed a black truck in the last couple of days? A Ford Ranger?"

"What's the license plate?"

I squeeze my eyes shut until I remember Uncle Bill's license plate number. I can hear her typing in the background.

"Yeah, yeah, we got it in a couple days ago."

My tongue is lead. It takes so much effort to ask, "Where did you find it?"

More typing. "I'm seeing here, hmm, out near Highway

95, a few miles up the 156 turnoff. Do you want to come in today to pick it up?"

That's way out in the desert. Uncle Bill wouldn't just abandon his truck out there, on the side of the highway.

"You'll need registration and a photo ID," she adds before I have a chance to respond to her first question.

"What if I'm not the owner?"

She sounds tired. "Then you'll need the owner to come with you."

"What if I don't know where he is?" Panic cracks my voice high and strained over the last words. The woman on the other end of the line goes quiet, and I wait for her to say something that will break the spell of dread that's suffocating me.

The typing picks up again. "Well, once you find him, have him come on down to the impound lot and pick it up. Towing fee's $150, plus $30 a day for every day it stays here."

"Can't I," I begin, but she interrupts me.

"I'm sorry, honey, but if it's not registered to you, you're out of luck. Is there anything else I can help you with?"

I don't even tell her no. Just hang up. Then I walk back home as the sun runs tracks of sweat the length of my spine. Uncle Bill isn't on some weekend trip. He's just gone. He left us, like Mom always said he would. Or something worse.

I won't let myself think about that. He's fine. He fucked us over, he abandoned us, but he's fine.

"Hey, honey," my mom says when I let myself in. "I made sandwiches."

She's washed her face and redone her lipstick, and her menopausal cherub's face is framed by a freshly washed blue sweatshirt. Minnie Mouse smiles wide and inviting from the front of it, mocking me.

She doesn't remember.

I bite into one of the sandwiches. An oil spill of grape jelly floods my mouth. "Thanks, Mom."

I take another bite and gag on the combination of dry bread and saccharine jelly. I want to hurt. I want to hurt in a way I've never hurt before, in a way that will strip me clean of the guilt and the terror long enough to think. I want to punish myself.

So I'll punish myself. What's the worst thing I can think of?

I chew the sandwich till it's mushy enough to swallow without choking. Then I excuse myself to the bathroom and run the shower so hot it steams up the mirror. Water pings off my exposed shoulders like tiny burning bullets. I kneel on the slick shower floor and retreat inside myself, reaching for cold iron and the beast beyond.

A small, useless voice inside me resists. Isn't it enough that I've given up my independence, that I'm maxing out my credit card to rent a car and drive alone into the desert, isn't it all enough suffering already?

A whimper. Chain rattles. I smother that voice and whisper, "Run."

Pain like a burning brand, like a thousand hot needles sliding into the divots of my spine. I bite my tongue and hope the remnants of the scream that leaks around it will be disguised by the hiss of the shower. My curse hurtles through the pathetic confines of my musculature, burrowing into creaking joints, seeking a weak spot where it can burst through. If I stumble, if I give in, it will pin my elbows back and thrust apart my ribs and I will no longer be hunger hiding in a human body, but a mutant creature primed for violence.

Stop. I crumple, sliding on my knees across the shower floor. Stopstopstop. My jaw warps. Saline floods my mouth.

It's too much.

It's what I deserve.

It only stops if I can stop it.

I grasp the chain at its root, a knot of iron deep in my chest. My senses are full of the wet smell of the air, the slip of water down my back, the brutal ache in my ligaments to run, to hunt, to show my teeth and what they were made for. Pressure like someone has pried open my chest, taken my heart in their hands and dragged me veins first from the bathroom, out of the apartment, across sidewalks and streets and highways till the scent of the desert surrounds me. As my nails turn to claws and my wrists twist in their sockets, I remember: Veer's driving to Reno today.

Not tomorrow, she'd said, her eyes liquid and hopeful. *I'm going up to Reno. But maybe next week.*

I thrust my will back inside myself, grip the chain and pull. I shouldn't call her. I rejected her. The beast bucks against me, ready to snap its jaws down on my throat. Don't think about her.

And don't call her. I want to, I'm desperate to have this reason to, and that's proof enough that I shouldn't.

Right?

When I catch my breath again, I'm on my hands and knees, vomiting up pale foam that swirls down the drain so fast I might have doubted it came from me at all, if not for the taste of stomach acid.

I already have my solution: a rent-a-truck I can't afford, and a long, lonely drive into the sweeping nothingness up north. Discoloration splotches my hips, crawling up my sides like finger marks in rotten fruit. I press my thumb into the bruise at the top of my thigh. It burns, blanching red to white like a flame turned up hotter the deeper I dig in.

As soon as I wrap myself in a towel, my phone's in my hand. She picks up on the first ring.

"Hey." She sounds breathless. She clears her throat, pitches her voice lower, casual. "Uh, how are you?"

"Fine." It slips out unthinking. Liar. And what would Veer say if I told her about my mom, my hunger, Uncle Bill's truck in an impound lot? Maybe my mom is onto something, after all. To be vulnerable with anyone but family is to show someone how to leave you. To open the door and push them through.

Veer clears her throat again. I've waited too long to respond.

"Is this about earlier?" I imagine her slouched over the arm of a beat-up couch or curled fetal on the floor of a beige-walled bedroom, worrying at her fingernails. "Because really, it's cool, I didn't mean to make you uncomfortable. It's just, I don't know, it seemed like we were . . ."

She trails off, and I'm quick to jump in. "It's fine. Seriously."

"Okay. Good. So what's up?"

Hang up now, Ellis. There's still time to stop this from becoming dangerous.

My fingers don't obey me. Neither does my tongue. "Are you driving up to Reno today?"

"Yeah. Why?" She barks out half a laugh, and I imagine her stretching her hands above her head, taking up space in triumph. "You looking for a ride?"

My throat is tight. "Maybe."

She chuckles, this one lower and quieter. Intimate. "Yes or no, Ellis."

There's still time. There's still time. And woven between my ribs is a craving that runs the length of me, and no matter how many cages I try to put myself in, I will always be an animal inside and I want, I want, I want.

"Yes," I say. "Please."

She's actually driving up to a little town northeast of Reno, she says, and Brian's place isn't too out of the way. She likes to do the drive up all at once, stay overnight at a highway motel, do her business in the morning, and get back to Vegas before it's dark. Same general idea as I had. She doesn't say what her business is, just that she's got family to see, and I try not to think too much about the motel.

"I need to drop my car off at the mechanic," I tell her. "Could you pick me up there?"

"Sure. Where is it?"

I give her the address and say I'll text her when I'm on the way, and she says that's great and laughs, and I feel hopeful for the first time in weeks.

My mom's in front of the TV when I head for the door a final time. After all that. She hugs a pillow as Rose regales Dorothy and Blanche about pickled herring. I look at her, and my mouth is filled with the bitter taste of the words I wish I could take back. When her mind finally fragments into so many pieces that she no longer recognizes me, what will be left of me? Who will I be without anyone to keep score of my flaws?

"Is it a good episode, Mom?" I ask.

She doesn't answer, just huddles deeper into the pillows. For a second, I wonder if she does remember and is just pretending. Then she mumbles, "Mm-hmm, Rose is my favorite," and I remember that's not how this works.

I palm our last two vials, nestle one in cold packs and bury it in my duffel bag, and pour the other into a red plastic cup from the back of the cabinet—*Shrimp Factory* is stamped on one side in white, along with a grinning cartoon shrimp—along with water and a packet of Emergen-C. Hopefully the fake citrus is enough to hide the smell of blood. Hopefully Joanne won't even notice it. I snap a photo of the cup and my mom's pill bottles, and text it to her so she knows what to look for when she comes by tomorrow. Then I kiss my mom on the cheek and tell her I'm going to work. She doesn't question it, and I tell myself the lie doesn't matter.

Only once Veer's dented Camry rolls to a stop in the car-shop driveway do I realize how much I didn't want to be alone for this.

The car chirps as its locks disengage. She's wearing battered black Wayfarers and a ratty Leonard Cohen T-shirt.

She rolls down the window. "Are you coming, or what?"

The car smells like diet soda and the foil insides of vending machine snacks. I suck in the recycled air and remember that dust is made of tiny fragments of dead skin, that I'm absorbing pieces of her just by breathing.

The sky is blue and endless as we turn onto the highway.

14

VEER TALKS WHILE SHE DRIVES. AS DIRT-WORN APARTMENTS give way to sprawling tract houses and cell towers disguised as palm trees, I learn that she's a Nevada girl, born and raised, that she grew up in the desert's blue-mountain embrace and spent her teenage years sneaking into the sad velvet of cash-strapped casinos and puking over the side of pickup truck beds. The houses dissolve into empty lots and construction sites, and I learn how she numbed the agony of adolescence by kissing girls who swore they just wanted to practice for their boyfriends, and slamming other kids into lockers. Always kids bigger than her, ones who'd punch back hard enough for her to feel it the next day. By the time she's told me about her first cigarette at sixteen, smoke kissed into her mouth by the prettiest girl in town, and how she's been trying to quit since her first week with EMS, the city is a distant memory and the mountains extend like welcoming arms along the endless line of Highway 95.

Veer pops another stick of cinnamon gum onto her tongue

and takes one arm off the wheel to stretch. Gold sunlight catches on the dips and crags of her arms, the shiny circular patches and uneven lines of raised tissue knit over long-healed cuts. She stretches wider, making a show of trying to sneak her arm around my shoulders like a teen at the movies, but she can't quite reach. Her fingers brush my cheek. For a moment, my curse and I are no longer adversaries, just two animals hoping that touch might linger, imagining the taste of her fingerprints.

We speed past red-scarred boulders and Joshua trees with limbs like broken fingers, and Veer tells me she's only left Nevada once, a weekend trip to Flagstaff with Kelsey. They took a detour through Sedona on the way back, slept parked on the side of the road in the back of Kelsey's car and woke up at five in the morning to hike up into the canyons.

"All those red rocks, washed out and whittled down, and the sunrise made them look so eerie, like aliens." She sounds enchanted, like she's left the highway's welcome mat of speed and asphalt and is kneeling in awe at the desert's altar. "Like angels, actually. Yeah. It was the most beautiful thing I've ever seen."

She slides her gaze to me, eyes warm and liquid, and an answering greed growls to life under my tongue. I want to tell her to pull over the car, to pull off her T-shirt, and to let me taste where her heartbeat pounds its rhythm into her bruises.

"Anyway," she says, and it's gone again—maybe it wasn't ever really there, maybe it's just my want and the blood in my duffel bag that I've waited too long to inject—"I know all my people are here, but I can't fucking die in Nevada."

Then she reaches for the stereo dial and turns the music all the way up.

I don't know where I'd want to die. With my mom and everything, it's hard to think too far ahead. The last time I drove this far, she was in the driver's seat and I was fifteen and tangled up inside. We drove from Colorado to Las Vegas without stopping, the seat belt working a welt over my collarbone. She wouldn't let me ride up front. You're just a kid, she said, and I believed it. I believed it, too, every time she swore we weren't running away. I was all she needed, and she was all I needed, and putting down roots was for people one season away from rot. The school system wasn't good enough, or the other kids' houses were too nice, or the teachers were taking too much of an interest in me. Even then, the boundary between real and not was hazy.

A lazy pile of sunset-colored rocks blurs past us, big enough to climb on. Big enough to crush me. I imagine my mom pacing the kitchen, *The Golden Girls* reduced to muffled gibberish in the background. I imagine her pinching the inside of her forearms as the bones of her face hum and warp, certain there's something she needs to do but not knowing what.

Veer reaches for another stick of gum. Cinnamon and sugar light up my sinuses. And what would my mom think about her?

She'd see Veer as an enemy, poised to tear me away from her. And she'd see me again as the ungrateful child, throwing myself at anyone willing to spirit me away from a mother I resent, from a life filled with bitterness.

Is that all I'm doing?

So what if it is. Can't that still be enough?

Maybe that's all Veer wants, someone desperate to cling to her. She hasn't tried to kiss me again. And I don't know, anymore, if who I should be is the same as who I want to be. It's been so long since I tried to separate the two. What if I no longer can?

The Joshua trees barely cast a shadow as they speed past. The wind doesn't have an answer.

"You hungry?" Veer asks as we pass a sign that promises "The International Car Forest," whatever that is.

"Yeah," I say without thinking. I'm hungry for so many things, and food is low on the list. But I could stretch my legs.

At Tonopah, we pull up in front of a wooden building that rises out of the asphalt wasteland around it like a mirage, shrieking *Hotel! Food! Casino!* in big block letters. A rusted mining cart and a statue of a rearing horse guard the entrance. As soon as we step inside, I'm choked by the scream of slot machines and the smell of fried oil.

The restaurant is carpeted in the same crimson-and-mustard paisley as the casino. The tables are wooden and too large for two, and there's no one else but us and a waitress who looks like she's more makeup than face. We order cheeseburgers and fries, and Veer fidgets with the drawstring on her basketball shorts as we wait. Her impatience smells like rancid vinegar. When her fingers drum on the scarred tabletop, same as they drummed on the polished plasticine at Rosy's, I recall the electric crackle of danger in the bar and the smell of her healing cuts as she bent over my car, of a cracked scab and the soft newness beneath. That cut on her hip is healed, but remnants of the bruise still linger yellow tinted in the crook of her elbow.

My hand moves toward it without my permission. Veer is watching the waitress wipe down the other tables, and she flinches when I touch her.

I draw back. Shouldn't have done that. "Sorry."

She smiles and tugs my hand back into the warm bend of

her arm. Her heartbeat flutters faintly under my fingertips. Or maybe it's mine. "You're good."

"What happened?" I don't mean to pry, only I'm already here with her, hours away from home, just the two of us and the desert. The waitress appears with two plates, and we snap apart like there's something to be ashamed of.

Veer ignores my question. Maybe she doesn't want to tell me.

I take a big bite of the cheeseburger and taste soil and char. The ketchup leaves a sugary slick on the roof of my mouth. Food never tastes quite the way it should for us, more texture than flavor, but even I can tell that this isn't exactly quality. I take another bite, try chewing it fast and swallowing faster, to see if that makes it easier.

Veer puts her burger down, checks over her shoulder that the waitress isn't looking, and grimaces. "Maybe we should have ordered something else."

"Not sure if that would help," I whisper back.

She laughs softly, the orange light from the old-fashioned chandelier making her eyes gleam. "Let me be an optimist."

I think about the taste of her broken skin, about pressing my tongue to the cut above her eye. Does she remember that? Did it scare her?

It scares me a little that I want to do it again.

Veer's water glass tinkles as she raises it to her mouth. When she puts it down again, she says, "A kid overdosed. Well, not really a kid, someone, like, our age. How old are you again?"

"Thirty-one," I reply automatically. What's she talking about?

"Oh." She smiles, rubs sheepishly at her temple. "Like my age, then."

I realize first that she's gone back to my question, that this is the start of what happened. And I realize second that I took it for granted that she was in her thirties, but she must be younger. I rewind through the life story she told me in the car and peg her for twenty-six. She just looks worn, lines around the eyes and a sad, sardonic edge to her smile. Is that what I look like too? Is that how she knew I had something dark in me?

"Anyway, we get up to this condo, and he's lying on the rug in front of the TV. Football player–looking dude, and his pupils, you know"—pinpoint, probably—"and hypoventilating. And his friend's totally freaking out, so I push the Narcan while Rodriguez preps the bag valve and keeps the friend calm." Her nose crinkles. "He's good at that. Guys respect him."

I wash another bite of the burger down with water. The ice makes my teeth ache.

"So he's on his side, I'm counting, friend's yelling at us, Rodriguez is doing his thing, and eventually I put him on his back again for oxygen and maybe a line, and, boom." She slams her hand on the table. It's not loud, but I still jump. "Up he pops, this huge guy who was barely breathing, like, a minute ago, and throws me right into the TV stand."

She grins like that's funny, and adds, "The best part is, he had a fucking katana up there, and I got this close to a surprise appendectomy."

Her voice and her face are making it a joke, but the oversalted burger can't hide the lingering fear on her breath.

"And then what?" I ask.

She shrugs. Pushes a couple of fries around on her plate. "And then we took him to the hospital. It's not his fault. If I woke up with a stranger in my face, I'd start swinging too."

She flags down the waitress. "I think I'll get the rest of this to go."

I ask for a box too, even though I don't plan to eat any more of it.

"Together?" The waitress asks, and Veer nods before I have a chance to ask for separate checks. In my lap, I dig the ridge of my thumb into the divot above my wrist joint.

Without warning, Veer leans across the table and sweeps my hair behind my ear. The edge of her fingernail scrapes my temple. It's still tender from my encounter with the freezer door. There's no bruise there, just a faint line of mottled red marks.

"Work got to you too?" Her voice is low, her eyes lingering on my hairline.

I want to shrink into my seat, but I force myself to stay still. Don't act ashamed. Don't make your mom sound like a monster.

"Got in a fight with the fridge." I hope I give it the same lighthearted ring as she gave her story. But her eyes sharpen like she knows there's something I'm not telling her.

The waitress runs her card and Veer signs, and I itch with uncertainty. What does she want me to do? What do I owe her now?

As we wind our way through the smoke-choked hotel hallway back to the parking lot, she leans in and mutters, "Not exactly where I envisioned taking you out, but hey. Could be worse, right?"

When she grins with all her crooked teeth, I wonder if I owe her at all.

15

THE HIGHWAY KEEPS STRETCHING ON FOREVER, AND Veer starts asking me questions.

"How long have you lived in Northtown?" is one.

"Since I was fifteen."

"Your folks still there too?"

"I live with my mom."

Should I explain that it's only temporary? What if she asks about the rest of my family? Do I tell her about Uncle Bill? Do I try to distract her with a summary of my father, which is, according to my mom, that he was a singer with bad eyesight and a worse haircut and enough charisma to make the whole party revolve around him, that he wanted a life with her and she picked up and left as soon as she could because that life would have ended in sharp fangs and ruin? Do I tell her that my mom is a liar, that I started to disbelieve that story when I was twelve and since then have simply stopped caring?

"You like it?" she asks when I don't keep talking.

"I guess." I want to say something trite, but I can't think of the right combination of words. I don't need to like it. That's not the point.

"Yeah," I correct, and focus on the mile markers zipping past the window. "She's good."

The wind picks up, tapping Morse code signals into the car frame. Betrayer, the gusts murmur to me. Shirker of duty. Ungrateful.

This is duty, I try to argue back. All of this is because of my mom, because she trashed a freezer full of blood in a few flailing minutes. I'm real because she needs me. What's the point of having no purpose?

I just wish I weren't so tired.

The congealing burgers in their Styrofoam prisons irritate my nose. I smell the grease soaked into cheap white buns, the cook's boozy breath, the waitress's constant hollowness.

Oh. That too. The hunger.

I glance at the gas gauge, but we're still three-quarters full. I pull up Google Maps and search for fast food ahead, an excuse to bury myself in a grimy bathroom and do what I need to do. The next hundred miles shows up a dead beige expanse.

Just ask her to pull over. Make something up. But every time I open my mouth, I end up spinning off into what-ifs. What if she refuses? What if she demands a reason to stop?

Veer reaches across me to tap the window. "Beautiful, huh."

Ahead, a pile of rocks juts proud and grinning, smoothed by wind and time into the shape of a sinking ship. The gold brown of the desert around it is dappled with sage-gray creosote bushes, their spindly shadows painted long and lovely by the sinking sun.

The desert and I aren't so different: both hiding brutality, both survivable at best.

There's an exit coming up. The pressure in my sinuses breaks through my paralysis. "Can we take a bathroom break soon?"

"Sure." Veer swerves onto the off-ramp. No hesitation. "Let's take it now. I want to climb these fuckers."

We bump onto a strip of dirt so apologetically narrow I'm not sure it even counts as a road. Veer bounds out of the driver's seat and into the calf-high scrub, and I mumble, "I'll go behind the car."

When her back's to me, I unzip my duffel bag and remove my last vial and a fresh disposable syringe. Crouched in the shadow of the car, the ridge of the door digging into my spine, I pop the cap off the vial. I can hear Veer scrabbling up the rocks.

Needle meets skin. Veer crows, "Ellis, look!"

Pull back. Stand up, wave. She's poised on the top of the pile, wriggling in time to music no one else can hear, or maybe just the wind. Silhouetted in the golden-hour glow, grinning so wide her face looks ready to split.

"Everything's bullshit!" She shrieks. "Nothing's worth dying for when the world is this beautiful!"

My chest squeezes in something like recognition. I give her a thumbs-up and drop back behind the car. Needle meets skin again and I'm lightning inside, and I want to live, yes, that's it, I want to live in a world as beautiful and solitary as this one, where there's no one to demand anything from me, just someone eager to share it.

My feet slip out from under me and I'm on my knees in the dirt, doubled over, incandescent, when Veer screeches suddenly, a high, panicked noise like a kicked animal.

Then a thud.

Surprise jolts the syringe from my hand. A sick pinch as it slides from the vein, drops into the dirt, still half-full. Shit. I wrench open the barrel and pour the remaining liquid into my mouth. I can't bring myself to waste it.

"Veer?" I call, to buy time as I tug a sweater from my bag and hide the dirty syringe and its curling plastic packaging. I hear movement, but she doesn't answer.

"Veer?" I'm shouting now, brush scraping my ankles. Her dark head pops up from behind the rocks.

"I'm good." She's a little out of breath. "Just, uh, lost my balance."

She dusts off her knees, and I smell broken skin somewhere under the dark billow of her T-shirt. Don't think about last time. Don't think about what you'd like to do to her, or your animal hunger.

"Did you hit your head?"

She crinkles her nose, looking sheepish. "Like, barely. I'm fine." She shakes her head like that proves it. "Look, Ma, no concussion."

"Okay. Can we just, like, double-check?"

Her grin falters. I shouldn't have second-guessed her. I wrap my arms around myself. The air gets cold fast in the desert, with the sun going down.

Then she pushes her hair off her forehead, and the wary snap to her gaze dissolves. Before I can stop her, she scrambles back up the rocks.

"Fine," she gloats, patting the smooth stone next to her. "Come up here and check."

The rock is gritty and harder to climb than it looks. Veer laughs a bit, watching me skid on the slick parts, but she reaches a hand down to keep me steady for the final stretch. I cling to her, feel the tendons flexing in her wrists.

"The doctor is in," I say solemnly as I settle next to her, and she laughs.

"Good news, Doc. There's only one of you, and you look great."

"So, not blurry." I haven't done this since nursing school. Veer probably knows how to test for concussion a lot better than I do.

She sticks her tongue between her teeth. "4K, baby."

I snort. Oh, hand-eye coordination. I remember that from the textbook.

"Touch my finger, then touch your nose." I hold it out in front of her face. She rolls her eyes, but taps my finger, her nose. I shift my finger side to side, and she does it again.

After a few times, she flicks my outstretched finger. "Want to do a balance test up here too?"

I laugh. "Fine, okay, you're not concussed."

"Told you."

She musses my hair, tongue still wedged under an incisor. She smells like scraped knees and the primal grit of the desert. She smells like that lemon hair gel I want to bury my nose in. This feels good, sitting on a rock in the middle of nowhere with her.

I like her, I realize with a nauseous twist. I really like her.

Liking is dangerous. With love, at least it's easy to know what's owed. There's no precipice of longing, no swirl of *what does she think* and *what if I'm wrong*, no constant kinetic whisper that if she leaned in, she'd be close enough to kiss me.

I want Veer to kiss me.

The sun blazes orange as it sinks into the mountains,

runny like an undercooked egg, furious as a funeral pyre. Its aftermath paints the mountains a wistful blue that fades suddenly into velvety blackness, and we're still up here, watching it happen. I'm not ready to come down just yet. But it's cold, and Veer's restless beside me. I hear, rather than see, her scramble down to safety.

"Just climb down where I did," she hisses out of the darkness. "It's not scary, I promise."

It is, though. The knot of hope tangled in my chest is scary, and the way it might gum up the lock on the cage inside me is terrifying. Also, I can't see. The toeholds I used to climb up are invisible in this light. I smell the creosote opening its arms to the night, but smell isn't going to stop me from a misstep that ends with my face smashed in.

Veer's phone lights up, giving shape to the rocks and casting her face in ghoulish black-and-white planes.

"Just a couple steps." She's softer now, less teasing, more encouraging. "Then I'll get you."

I take a few tentative steps, then end up sliding on my ass the rest of the way, almost directly into Veer's outstretched arms. I freeze for a second, not sure whether I'm supposed to use her as a step stool or what, but she's already wrapping one arm around my lower back and the other around my knees and I guess it's a princess carry.

When my arms settle around her neck, I find the phone light is very bright and our faces are very close. She's also, I notice, very strong.

Then my feet are on the ground and she's kissing me, quiet and tentative, like groping for a handhold in the dark. She pulls back, and I chase after her, pushing my fingers into the softness at the back of her neck. This, too, is what I want, the freedom to close my eyes, to kiss her slow without worrying that life will interrupt us.

When we're done, she leans into me, her forehead meeting my cheek.

"Let's get back to the car," she mumbles. "There's a hot shower waiting for us an hour down the road."

A hot shower, and a motel room, and I don't know what else, but I want to find out.

We don't talk much the rest of the drive, but Veer settles her hand on my thigh and leaves it there until we pull into the parking lot of the motel.

16

VEER GETS US A ROOM WITH TWO TWIN BEDS.

It smells like vanilla body spray and bleach smeared over vomit and cigarette smoke. The side-by-side beds gaze impassively into the black mirror of an old TV. I swing my duffel bag onto the foot of the bed farthest from the door.

I'm not sure what the room means, or if it means anything at all.

Veer hasn't quite looked at me since we parked, a handful of sideways glances instead of her full-bore high-beam stare. Still, there's a deliberateness to the way she sets her stuff—a battered backpack, massive silver water bottle, and a baseball hat embroidered with *Off Duty, Save Yourself*—down on the other bed, like she knows exactly where I am without having to look.

But she doesn't talk. And I don't quite know how to fill the silence.

I want to. Or, I think I want to. What does she think of me? What does she want? What is she waiting for me to do?

I pull off my shoes without bothering to untie them. Desert dust has crept into the creases in the leather, making them look even more beat up than usual. Out there, the wind and the cold and the fading light made my mom feel very far away. Now, I can't stop thinking about her.

Veer coughs, kicks off her sneakers, and suddenly I can't hold on to all of it alone anymore.

"My mom's sick." It comes out of my mouth before I can think it through. "She's losing her mind."

Veer freezes in place, hunched over, one hand pulling her foot free from her sock. White with pink polka dots. Then she snaps back to life again, straightens. Rubs the back of her neck.

"Losing her mind?" She says it carefully, like she doesn't want to assume.

"Alzheimer's. Early onset, I'm not *that* old." I laugh a bit, but it sounds hollow. She does the kind thing and doesn't laugh along.

"I'm sorry."

"Don't be. It's just, sometimes I feel like I'm losing my mind too."

I sit down too fast on the bed, and it squeals in protest. I thought sharing secrets was supposed to feel good, but all I can think about is how now there's no taking it back.

Veer slides next to me and picks up one of my hands by the pad of the thumb, her grip loose enough that I could shake her off if I wanted to. "It's just you and her?"

"Yeah." Well, there's Uncle Bill too, but it's not the same thing. And he's gone now.

"She loves me," I say, because that will realign my compass. "She loves me so much. And I try to love her. I try so hard, okay?" My voice cracks, betraying me, and I swallow to hide it. "But sometimes I just want to quit."

Wouldn't it be nice to dig inside myself and sift out all the things I owe, until I find the gleam of what I want. Wouldn't it be nice to wonder what will happen tomorrow instead of already knowing.

"Forget it," I add quickly. "I know that's a messed-up thing to say."

I only feel Veer shiver because I'm pressed against her side.

"I don't think it's messed up," she says. Then she sucks in air and mutters, "I'm gonna shower."

She doesn't wait for me to acknowledge it before sweeping a plastic bag out of her backpack and heading for the bathroom. The door slams behind her like a slap in the face. I stare at my murky reflection in the darkened TV screen. I should have held my tongue.

As the shower sputters to life, I fish the used syringe and empty vial from their cocoon in my sweatshirt and place them side by side in one of the motel-provided paper cups. I wrap it all in a washcloth and bury it at the bottom of the trash can. I try sitting on the bed again, but I hate the way it squeaks whenever I move. It feels too much like I'm waiting for Veer to come back, so I slide onto the ground, then stretch out on my back. The muscles around my spine release one by one as my wary animal paces behind its prison door. I think back to kneeling in the shower, the way it leapt at my call. The agony, like I've never felt before. Sudden temptation flutters at my fingertips. To let my animal's snarl line up with my teeth, to touch for a second the inhuman depths of my own power, and then to cage it again. How's that for control?

I dig my fingers into the carpet, tracing the faded pattern of red swirls, gone soft-edged and brownish with wear. The shape and the color, together, look a little like bloodstains. I remember the dark patch congealing in Uncle Bill's office, and for a second, all the air is sucked out of my lungs.

I pinch the skin on my stomach, where a bruise stretches wretched under the seam of my jeans. Don't think about it. It's not real.

When the shower stops, I pinch myself again, then scramble back onto the bed.

Veer comes out of the bathroom, hair slicked back and dripping, the excess water running rivulets down her neck and shoulders into the towel wrapped around her chest. It's long enough to cover her whole torso, but short enough to expose shins and knees and thighs. There are more of the tick-mark scars on the insides of her legs, and a yellow-green quilt of faded bruises ring one knee.

"Hi," she says, peeking at me from under her brows.

"I have to shower too," I blurt out. I haul my entire bag to the bathroom and run the water as hot as it goes.

Once I'm done scrubbing the desert off my skin, it occurs to me that I've done the wrong thing again. I should have kissed her, not run away. I lather the length of my arms before the sliver of motel soap snaps in half and vanishes down the drain. Veer left a bottle of travel-size shampoo in the corner of the shower. I snap it open and pour a bit into my hand before I can think twice about it. As I use it to wash the rest of my body, I wonder if she'll notice that I smell like her.

No, she won't. She'll notice my purpling wrists, my cracked toenails, the broken blood vessels spattering my stomach like spider bites. She'll notice the stains my leaping curse punched into my hips, my shins, my spine, a canvas of black and blue that should remind her to be afraid.

I don't want her to be afraid of me. But I couldn't bear her pity either.

The showerhead sighs and the water pressure slows. Maybe that's a sign. I don't want to get out. I don't know how to face Veer. I want her to look at me and see the sharp edges and sharper claws, not the facade those things hide behind.

When I emerge from the bathroom, Veer is sitting on my bed, changed into an oversize tank top and tiny green shorts. She shifts, and the mattress squeaks. "Hey."

"Hey." I slip down onto the bed, not right next to her but close enough to know that she smells like mineral water and scented dryer sheets. I want to be closer. I want to know how each of her vertebrae taste.

"Look." She pulls back one of her tank top straps to expose the front of her shoulder. A length of skin scraped raw from her fall. She leans forward, and I smell brake dust and cinnamon gum, hotel soap disintegrating between fingers, things that are easy to feel and hard to say.

"I'm sorry," I whisper.

Her face tips up and her eyes swallow me, huge and dark and luminous. "Don't be."

I slide over, and as our thighs meet, she tenses, barely visible, a tiny ripple of tightening muscles. I wait for her to grip me by the throat or push me to the floor, but she doesn't. Just leaves that raw expanse stretched before me in expiation.

I lean in and surrender to it.

My tongue traces the constellation of marks, and fireworks light in my throat. Her free hand meets my shoulder, strong fingers digging into the ridges of my collarbones, plowing toward the base of my neck. I'm enveloped by the rich, reckless heft of her blood, like a burning building, like a blooming flower, as she grips my hair and guides me off the edge of the bed. Cheap carpet scrapes my knees, and Veer pushes back the hem of her shorts to expose new tracts of raw pink and bruise yellow and I bend my mouth again to lick her wounds.

"Ellis," she gasps, and I wish my tongue had a razor edge so I could cut my way into her, so I could make her veins smell like my sweat and devotion.

She shifts, calves wrapping around my torso. I bend to her again, mouth no longer seeking blood but a different kind of wetness, and for the first time in too long I know exactly what I want.

Later, I lie on my back and examine the motel ceiling. Its uneven maroon is marred by peaks and valleys of hastily slapped-up stucco. You could probably quiz everyone who's had this room for the last six months, and they wouldn't remember the color.

"I'm scared," I whisper to the ceiling.

Veer stirs slightly and presses her face into my neck. "Hmm?"

"Nothing."

Her forehead nudges my shoulder. I wish we could go back to when it was my teeth and her skin, when the animal in my bones knew what to do.

"Come on," she urges. Not a demand. A plea. "Tell me."

If I say no, the moment will end. I know it, and she knows

it too, and that's why her voice sounds like that, like she's holding on to the end of a fraying rope. She wants it to stay us, together in the cocoon of flaky paint and someone else's linens, the world past the dead bolt dim and unreal.

I want it too.

"My mom." It takes me a while to find the words. "What if I'm glad when she's dead? I told her I hated her, right before I left. She smashed up my car, and I was pissed and I just . . ."

Veer says nothing, doesn't move, just blows out a long, low breath.

"I think my uncle's dead too." It's the first time I've said it out loud, and it's a relief, even though it's also another piece of me carved off, another hollow space dug out.

Veer rolls over to face me. "Shit. I'm sorry."

"He did a lot for me, and I'm grateful, but I don't know. He'd say he loved me, but he always had some catty remark when I did something he didn't agree with. Which was like, all the time. I just tolerated him and I thought that was it, but then he kind of disappeared, and . . ."

"Disappeared? Like, skipped town?"

"I don't know. Maybe, I guess. But the same day we stopped hearing from him, someone broke into his house. There was blood in his office. Like he'd been in a fight."

Veer's fingers brush the inside of my wrist. "Did you call the cops?"

Our family doesn't call the police. They wield cages like weapons, and once we're in cages, things always get innumerably worse.

"Whoever broke in didn't take anything," I say, because I can't explain that to her. "I doubt the cops would help."

"Yeah," she says ruefully, "maybe."

"Anyway, he was into some shady shit. Nothing big, but, you know. Wouldn't want to get him in trouble."

"Sure." She squints, considering. "If it makes you feel any better, people who are into shady shit are usually pretty resilient. He's probably halfway to Mexico or something."

"His truck got picked up on the side of the highway. Way out in the desert, abandoned."

The sheets rustle. She doesn't have an answer for that.

"Maybe he is okay, but I honestly . . ." I draw in a shaky breath. When did my throat get so tight? "I don't think so. But I still keep getting ready to pick up the phone to call him, or think I'm going to drive to his house, or, you know, and then I remember he's not there anymore. And I just want to cry. I miss him. But I never missed him when he was around. Sometimes I think I do hate my mom, but what if when she goes, it's just like my uncle, only worse?"

When she goes. As if I'll have the gift of such distance, as if it won't be me and a kitchen knife.

Veer's fingers close over mine. "It probably will be."

I jerk my hand away. That's not what she's supposed to say. She's supposed to promise me it won't be, supposed to go for the easy answer, supposed to lie.

Then I catch myself. Is that really what I want? Or is it this, the brutal blow of honesty, the relief of someone else saying, *Yes, yes, you're right to be afraid, and when this thing you dread comes true, you'll have to learn to live with it. It will be just as bad as you imagine, and still you'll survive it.*

Veer pushes herself to sit, twining her arms around her knees. "You know, I was glad when my dad died."

I sit up too, surprised. She'd talked for hours in the car and never once mentioned her dad. I hadn't noticed it at the time.

"I'm sorry," I say automatically.

Discomfort lances across her face. "Don't be. My brother bashed his face in with a baseball bat when I was eleven, I saw the whole thing and it probably fucked me up for life, but trust me, Ellis: he fucking deserved it." She flops back onto the bed, swaying with the squeak and bounce of the decrepit mattress. "Maybe you will be glad when she dies. Family's complicated."

She blinks slow and deliberate, and I breathe her deep into my lungs, smell her furious mix of wrath and regret.

"That's, um." She blinks again, swallows, stares up at the ceiling. "I'm going to visit him, actually."

"Your brother?"

She nods.

"He lives in Lovelock?"

Her eyes flick toward me, daring me to laugh, then away again. "He's in prison."

"For, um . . ." Is it wrong to ask?

"No, not for my dad. That was self-defense." A dry polyester rasp as her legs scrub up and down the top sheet. "He got into some fucked-up shit after, though. Held up a gas station, ended up in a youth center. When he got out, my mom put him in one of those, you know, go-out-to-the-desert-with-ex-military-fuckos. Troubled-teen camp, or whatever. He got out a couple days before my junior prom. He was supposed to . . ."

She wraps her arms around herself, fingers drumming at her pockmarked triceps. "Anyway. He didn't come home, and I was so pissed because I'd gotten all done up in this sparkly blue dress with my hair curled, so I left him this long, nasty voicemail about how I never wanted to see him again and he was such a fuckup and, you know, and my mom's all mad at me, saying it's not his fault, and I mean, now that I'm older I get it, but she was such a pushover all my life and always wanted me to be her little dress-up doll baby girl and I just . . ."

Another long breath. "Next time I saw him was at his arraignment. He tried to rob a casino with a fuckin' box cutter. Blinded the floor manager."

She grabs me without warning, fingers closing over mine with such force that I wonder if she wants to break them. "He wasn't always a fuckup. I know I should just be grateful for what he did and, like, forgive him for all the other bullshit. People talk like forgiveness is so easy, but it's not. So, no, I don't think you're a horrible person for thinking, you know, whatever about your mom. I wish I was better at letting things go too."

"Family's complicated," I echo.

Veer raises our intertwined hands to her mouth and kisses my knuckles one by one. "It's not fair."

"Nothing's fair." They're my mom's words. But they're also true: there's no balance to any of this, no reason. It just is.

"Do I scare you?" Veer murmurs.

I pull back without thinking. Her grip tightens into something demanding. Her front teeth trace the curves of my tendons.

"Or"—she twists my hand, so the pad of my thumb sits between her canines—"do you wonder what I'd be like, if it had been me with the bat?"

"No." I wish she'd bite down. I wish she'd eat me alive.

"It should have been."

"Veer."

Her nostrils flare. "If he did something, I could have."

"You were eleven."

"And my brother was fifteen. Come on." She nips my thumb. "You know the most pathetic thing? It never even occurred to me that I could. Or should. I thought that was just what it was like to be a kid."

An abyss in the shape of my mom's voice clogs my throat.

"We have to take the good with the bad," she'd hissed. "We take care of each other, no matter what. That's what families do."

She'd said that on the drive to Vegas, that first one, while I hunched over a math workbook in the back. She knew I didn't want to leave Colorado Springs, and maybe that was why she kept talking for hours about how good it would be, how happy Uncle Bill would be to see us. How this was the start of a new life. Maybe that was why she accused me of deliberately forgetting my workbook at a rest stop. Maybe that's why she still remembers that one moment, that one story, even as the rest of my childhood fades.

I don't think she remembers the look on Uncle Bill's face when we pulled into his driveway that first time. The disappointment, and resignation. But I do. It became a part of my armor: the understanding that it was always like this for us. For all of us.

"Does that freak you out?" Veer's voice is casual, her eyes pinpoints of intensity.

"No."

Her jaw tightens. "It should. I'm all fucked up inside, Ellis. I keep trying to unfuck myself, but it's, like, built in. Like there's poison in my blood."

I press my lips to the base of her thumb and look into the black holes of her eyes. "I'm not scared of being poisoned."

Veer catches me by the chin, and for a second, I'm scared I've said too much. Then she pulls me into her and kisses me like a tidal wave, like an unfurling of compressed pain into my mouth. When she lets me go, I'm gasping.

"You're one deep, dark, scary girl, Ellis," she whispers. Her fingers find the bruise on my hip and press, not hard enough to hurt, but hard enough to feel her presence. "I've never met anyone quite like you."

I shiver. I'm supposed to smell danger, to panic that she's feeling around the edges of the truth and that my throat aches to tell her the rest. I'm so tired of secrets and manipulation. I'm so tired of being alone.

It's too much to grapple with, this and my mom and Uncle Bill and the future, and suddenly my throat is filled with metal spikes and each breath catches on them and I will myself not to cry, but my eyes sting and then it's too late to stop. Veer's arms are around me, her fingers stroking evenly across the back of my skull, and I cling to her as she pulls me in tighter and tighter, the vise of her arms the only thing keeping me from fracturing.

"Hey," she murmurs into my hairline. "Fuck everybody, okay? Fuck love."

I sniff, then laugh, horrible hiccuping sobs that feel like absolution.

"Fuck love," I repeat. It feels good. "Everyone I love makes me feel like shit."

"Goddamn right." Veer laughs and kisses me again.

We fall asleep like that, tangled up in each other, and I dream of things I don't remember.

17

I WAKE UP FIRST. VEER IS PRESSED INTO MY SIDE, ONE arm flung over my chest. The easy hum of cars outside like a white noise blanket.

Today, I'll bury my worries about my mom and focus on the thing I know is real: Brian, and the menace of walking into a stranger's house and hoping you can trust him.

Pale daylight peeks around the edges of the curtains. It catches on the comforter wrapped around my legs, turning its cheap quilted seams into the pitted scars of a flood-carved canyon. I scan the room, making a semiconscious inventory of our things. My duffel bag's zipper-toothed smirk. Veer's tank top puddled at the foot of the bed.

The corner by the door looks funny. It's too dark, like there's something there the sunlight can't penetrate. The hairs on my arms stand to attention.

A noise like a camera flash, and day-bright yellow blots my vision. A four-legged figure materializes for a moment in the glare. Worm-ridden muscle pulls taut over its bent-back bones, fleshless lips curling to reveal rows and rows of saw-edged teeth.

Then, just as fast, it's gone.

The bed is too small. I'm trapped by the sheets, caged by the insistent contact of Veer's body. I need to move. I try to lift my head, but my neck screams in protest. My leg is cramping. Her arm is an anvil pushing down on my lungs. I can't breathe, dread is folding me smaller and smaller and soon I won't even exist, I'll be dry bones ready to be snapped in half, to crumble to dust because there's nothing left of me to destroy.

Veer stirs.

"Good morning," she mumbles, and kisses me, and my panic ebbs and it's all just sheets and skin again.

The motel coffee tastes like moldy cardboard. We stop at Taco Bell, and Veer gets cinnamon twists for breakfast. When she twines her fingers with mine over the top of the car console, the sugary grit rubs off on my knuckles.

We drive, Veer talks, we stop again for gas and more coffee. This cup tastes like aspartame and fumes. The road rumbles restless under our tires as she tells me about her brother, about their childhood scars and how night after night of hauling bodies softened her anger toward him. She emails him every week, but this is her first visit in a while. In too long. She's nervous about what he might say to her, and more nervous that she won't know what to say back.

I tell her about Uncle Bill, about his dog-shit yard and the chemical smell of his hands. How he liked his instant coffee, how he was in a bad garage rock band when he was a teenager, how he ditched my mom and how she found him again. How he'd stop just short of saying that he resented having us around, but how I glimpsed it out of the corner of my eye sometimes, how I smelled it on sweltering, windless days, a scent halfway between brake dust and watered-down whiskey.

And I tell her about my mom. About her pink lipstick and her favorite shows, about all the things she lies about. Finally, I tell her about the freezer door and the smashed windshield and how it felt to tell her I hated her, to know it was the truth and still wish I'd cut my own tongue out instead of saying it.

Veer listens, quiet, her hand on mine, and maybe she's getting ready to say something, but the GPS interrupts. "Turn right on Coal Canyon Road."

We turn, and turn again, and then we're there.

Desert gives way to parking lot gives way to a low, brutal concrete slab with a glass entrance. The facade is painted a deep, vibrant blue, the opposite of the desert's brown-green haze. Maybe that's on purpose, the state of Nevada's big fuck-you reminder that its desire for subjugation is stronger than the earth's barbarity. Still, the mountains loom yellow and silent behind it as if to say, *Go ahead and try. No walls can ever keep me out, no guard towers or barbed wire or electric doors can keep me in.*

Veer squeezes my hand. I smell her deodorant and the stick of gum long chewed-out and stuck under her tongue, and underneath both, I smell her fear and uncertainty.

"Okay," she says, like she's nerving herself up. "I'll be done in an hour, max. Are you cool to take the car, then pick me back up?"

"Yeah," I say quickly. I had assumed she'd want me to wait here, and drive together to Brian's, but this is better. Safer.

She nods, like she's trying to convince herself too. "Call me when you're on the way back. Actually, can you turn on location sharing?"

I toggle it on and she does too. Then she squares her shoulders and jerks the keys out of the ignition. She's already halfway out the door as she shoves them into my hand. She freezes, suddenly, dips back, but I react too slow and her kiss presses into the side of my mouth.

I want to try again—and again, and again, and again—but the car door's already slammed behind her. She doesn't look back as she disappears into the glass doors' hungry jaws.

I drive eighty all the way to Brian's.

The beauty of the desert is in how it eats. It gnaws at house paint and car doors, whips sharp fingernails over shins, it licks and chews and takes its due. The desert has carved crimson gouges into Brian's chain-link fence, eroded the once-red flag of his mailbox, suffocated a front yard full of junked auto parts and a half-demolished pickup that might have started out blue, a long time ago. The house is the same brown as the dead grass and the desert beyond, and the only thing between me and it that isn't coated in dust is a big black-and-white laminate sign.

This house is guarded by God and a gun, it reads. *If you trespass, you'll meet them both.*

I squint at the pulled-shut curtains. Baby blue with little eyelets at the bottom, faded white in the middle where the sun's strongest. I figure the God part is bullshit. The gun part, I'm not so sure.

"You here?" Brian demands when I call him on the Nokia, still standing halfway between the street and his door.

"Yeah." Be polite, Ellis. "Yes."

"Did your uncle not teach you to knock, or what?"

I try to remember how I used to talk to Uncle Bill, but my brain's a sieve and my body's something worse and I can't playact the way I used to. At least my feet pick up and walk me toward the door. I apologize into the phone and stuff it back into my pocket and knock. The door was painted green, once. Now it's just as brown as everything else.

On the other side, one, two, three dead bolts slam, and the door squeals open with the smell of old paper and overcooked sausage.

"Shit," Brian wheezes through three inches of opening, like he's afraid that if he swings the door wide, the desert will get its claws over the threshold. "Anyone ever tell you that you look a lot like him?"

"No." People only ever cooed over the similarities between me and my mom. *You could be sisters*, they'd say. My mom loved that one. "But thanks."

Brian pulls the door open just enough for me to slip through. He's a big guy, thick neck and red forearms striped with dark hair. Tan T-shirt with an American-flag-like pattern on the front, ball cap pulled low even inside. Two broken-backed couches crowd his living room, one dark leather with cracks in the cushions, the other draped in gold tassels and spinsterly floral with a skirt hanging to the floor. Gas station figurines of dragons and fairies watch in neat rows from the mantel. One at the end wears a long, black plastic cloak with a sword held to its forehead, part grim reaper, part evil wizard. The coffee table sags under the weight of stacked paperbacks: *Scats and Tracks of the Rocky Mountains, God Emperor of Dune, The Art of Keeping Your Ass Alive.*

"Water?" Brian calls over his shoulder as we move from the living room into the kitchen. "Might have a beer in the fridge too, if you're a beer gal."

There's a fan plugged in on the counter. I don't think he has air-conditioning.

"Water would be nice." My folding cooler flails like a limp rag under my arm. "If you don't mind. Do you have ice?"

He turns around as I struggle to snap the cooler into something vaguely rectangular. His eyes are a very pale blue.

"Have a drink first," he says.

His fridge hums with the same muted menace as the pitchfork-wielding crowd in a monster movie. He brandishes a glass, and in response, the fridge door spits a stream of faintly orange water.

"Got my own well out back," Brian explains as he sets the glass on the table in front of where he wants me to sit, then pulls a can of 7UP out from under the sink for himself.

"Neat." The table is plastic and sunwarped. The water smells like minerals and horse shit. Tastes like it too.

"I've got three acres. All the neighbors moved to Reno or Salt Lake. Couldn't handle the isolation. Me, I like it." His grin reveals very straight teeth. A twist, a crack, and the 7UP can hisses weakly. "Your uncle ever teach you to handle a gun?"

"Um." Would it be worse to say yes, or no? "No?"

Brian shakes his head and takes a long drag at the can. "He should have. Vegas is fucked up these days. Junkies everywhere, homeless begging on every corner, real fucked-up sex trafficking shit."

Now I remember what it was like talking to Uncle Bill. Biting my tongue to keep him comfortable. Or at least trying to. I think of the desperation of the meth-jittered couples who come through the ED, arms scratched up and voices hoarse, and of the patients who come in an ambulance because they're too poor to get to the doctor before their bodies give out on them. I think of my mom's failing mind and our dusty apartment building, and I wonder when the last time was that Brian even left his property, much less drove all the way to Vegas.

"Everywhere's fucked up."

"True." His pale eyes drift toward the kitchen window and stay there, cast colorless by the equally colorless desert light. "I can teach you to shoot, if you want. Go out back, shoot some empty cans."

He tips the rest of the soda into his mouth and flicks the can onto its side. It rolls disconsolately across the table.

"Maybe next time."

Brian laughs, sort of, and taps his forehead. "Sure, I get you. Stranger danger."

I should probably protest, but I don't quite have it in me. "How do you know Uncle Bill?"

He itches one of his thick red arms. "Found him through the map. Just like everyone else."

I have no idea what that's supposed to mean. After a second of silence, he slaps his hands on his thighs and clears his throat with a snap like a pocketknife unfolding. "Right. Never mind. Your mom is Bill's crazy sister."

I can't help rising to the bait. "Did Uncle Bill say that?"

"No. Nobody said anything." He frowns like he's probably lying, and mutters something that sounds like "Crazy behavior is crazy behavior."

"Nobody's crazy." My eyes catch on my reflection in his toaster, my face stretched long and formless like taffy on a pull. "She's sick. Did Uncle Bill tell you that?"

His eyes gleam. "Sick? Sick how?"

I shift in my chair. In the toaster, my face scrunches into

a copper-colored tomato as my neck warps and narrows. So easy to get your jaws around. I don't have to tell Brian anything if I don't want to.

"Brain stuff. She doesn't always know what she's doing. It's fine."

Brian's brows rise. "Yeah, sounds fine."

When I don't respond, he shrugs. "Well, let's head down, I'll get you stocked up."

I stand. My water glass is still mostly full. "Down?"

"To the basement." Brian shoves his way out of his own chair with a squeak. "What, you think I'd set everything up here, where just anyone can look in the window and see?"

I decide not to mention how he said all his neighbors moved away.

As I follow him through the living room, he pauses to flick some dust off a plastic woodland fairy with flowing brown hair and huge tits, part of the fantasy menagerie on the mantel.

"Hey," he says suddenly. "You ever seen a car wreck?"

I remember the little girl and her mother and their flipped car. "I see a lot of people who get in them."

Suspicion sparks in his eyes. "Highway patrol?"

"Nurse. Emergency department."

He relaxes. "Oh. That's good. Then you'll be fine."

I fix my eyes on the faded spots of the couch's floral upholstery. My mom loves rose prints like this one. Not the flowers themselves—*They smell like cough syrup, and thorns? So annoying, who came up with those*—but her closet overflows with flowery designs and tiny rosettes.

I miss her. Or I'm worried about her. It's hard to tell the difference.

On my way in, I was too busy noticing Brian to notice what

he had in his entryway. Now that I'm used to his gas-station-meets-country-grandma-meets-bushcraft weirdo aesthetic, it's hard not to notice that one thing doesn't fit: a painting not much bigger than a sheet of printer paper, framed in silver and hung on a door that looks like it should lead to a coat closet. On it, two hyena-like creatures twist around each other, each one's bared fangs aiming for the other's throat. It's designed almost like a coat of arms, with a motto inked underneath. *Defend and advance.*

I haven't smelled blood anywhere in the house. Another thing I should have noticed earlier.

A broken-in suede bomber jacket hangs by its collar on the doorknob, but Brian nudges it aside to reveal a thick combination lock that he opens seemingly by touch. Past the door is a set of uneven concrete stairs. Naked bulbs dangle from the ceiling.

He's one of us, I remind myself. He's going to help me.

The air shifts from desert stifling to sterile cold on our way down. It's just a concrete room down there, with a big utility sink, a banged-up trash can, and a steel door set into one wall. The same insignia from upstairs is burned into the door, so large that the hyena creatures' heads are bigger than my own.

Brian pulls a bundle from a plastic bin balanced on the side of the sink. "Put these on."

I recognize the rubbery blue of nitrile gloves. A surgical mask is tucked between them.

"Got a hairnet around here somewhere too," he mumbles.

I pull on the gloves too fast and the elastic snaps back, a bite at the inside of my wrist. The mask smells papery to the point of sweetness, drowning out any other lingering smells that might reach me down here. It's a familiar scent, the mask, one I anchor myself to at work if a trauma patient rolls in unexpectedly, but smelling it here feels strange. Brian hands me a hairnet, then dons one himself and reaches for the keypad set into the concrete next to the door.

The keypad wails, the door disengages with a sterile hiss, and I don't know exactly what I'd expected to see behind it, but I know that I didn't expect this.

"Jesus Christ." It escapes me before I can fully understand what I'm looking at.

The space runs the length of the house, maybe even longer, but it's got more in common with a hospital lab than the dusty rabbit warren upstairs. No doors, just scrubbed-down walls and support pillars, shelves and sinks and storage. All clean. All sterile.

All white, except for the specimens.

Twenty, thirty tanks—empty aquariums, I realize, as I step closer—each filled with a lump of tissue and flesh and pinched-off vascular systems. Plugged into water pumps and toy motors and lab parts, some shuddering like plates of Jell-O, some pulsing with tiny heartbeats. Only they aren't hearts. They aren't any organ I recognize.

The room smells like wet paint and antibacterial spray, and even through my surgical mask the blood and the flesh and the mutant tissue smells so good I have to dig my nails into my palms to keep from falling to my knees.

Above his mask, Brian's pale eyes flash with malicious satisfaction. "You thought I was just some survivalist nut, didn't you."

"Of course not," I lie. But how could I have expected this? It's not the false rise and fall of lungless torsos that disturbs me, or the way the sutures can't quite hold some of the pieces together, leaving tissue bulging out between them like a pink stomach pressed to prison bars. It's the single-minded calculation of it. How long ago did he plan this lab out? How many days has he worked toward it, piece by tiny piece?

"Took me years to get set up," Brian says, like he read my mind. "Isn't it beautiful?"

It's true. I can't help but admire how uniform his sutures are.

As I drift after him, my gaze catches on a stack of textbooks. These are very different from the books upstairs. *Smith's Recognizable Patterns of Human Malformation. Biomaterials for Artificial Organs. Principles of Tissue Engineering,* third edition.

Brian says something else, but the mask muffles it. "Evolution," he repeats. "Right?" He shuffles around the tanks, removing lids, swirling pinkish liquid with a slender metal rod. "We're not like them. Sure. But the question is *why*, right? Why. Now, I'm not saying anyone *made* us. What I'm saying is, what are we going to make of ourselves?"

I watch as a mass the color and texture of raw chicken breast inflates, the glistening membrane around it growing translucent as it swells. Then, abruptly, it deflates again. Brian stops and turns, faster than I would have expected of someone his size.

"Us." He digs a thumb into his chest. "We're what's next. We're stronger, we're better adapted. We're evolution in progress."

"Are we?" Our entire lives, all our choices, revolve around ensuring we're able to feed. Every day. Every single day. And there's always the chance that tomorrow something changes, your uncle disappears, and your lifeline is gone.

Brian could change that, with what he's building here. But I get the feeling that's not where this is heading.

"I thought you had to be kind of smart to be a nurse," he

grumbles. “If I cut you, it heals. If you don’t eat for a week, you’ll be miserable, but you’ll survive. All we actually need to live is a little blood. Which is hard to come by, sure, but that isn’t proof we’re weak. It’s proof that we’re living in a world designed to keep us weak. It’s not our fault we’ve been set up to fail. Think about it. If they knew what we could do to them, we’d get all the blood we asked for, and not just that. We’d get the respect we deserve. Oh yeah. Just imagine.”

“They should know,” he adds as he snaps another lid back into place. “They should be afraid.”

A couple of weeks ago, a fourth-grade girl came into the ED with a concussion. Fell off the monkey bars funny. She had such long eyelashes, and she looked at me like I was a snake and she was the mouse I’d hypnotized right before devouring it. I wonder if that’s what I look like now, to Brian.

“Well, I.” I stop myself. We need him. “I don’t know.”

“This”—he nods at the aquariums—“is temporary. Once I’ve got the process perfected, that’s when the next phase starts.”

“It’s not . . .” How to phrase it? “Is it safe? To inject?”

It must be, right? How else could he survive living out here all alone? But I don’t like the sound of an imperfect process.

Brian’s brows draw down. I imagine a scowl growing under his mask. “Do I look like an idiot? Of course it’s safe. I’m not some jerk who watches YouTube videos about science. I’ve been doing this for twenty years. More, actually. I got into tissue engineering when I was in grad school, got a PhD, worked in a lab, whole nine yards. Administration would tell you I had a mental breakdown at the end, but really, I just decided I was through, and ready to come out here and do the rest on my own.” The mask muffles his chuckle, but I get the gist: pride, cynicism, superiority. “Like I said, it’s almost ready. And then, well, I've got my own water, lots of scrap metal, plenty of land. I'm going to be smart about who gets to share it, obviously. Only the best evolved of us, the toughest. The ones who get it. Now that's the kind of community worth building."

I remember the motto upstairs. *Defend and advance.* Is he, in this moment, trying to determine if I'm one of the good ones? One of the ones who get it, who want to—what? Build a militia of creatures like us? Get the respect we deserve?

"What's your mom got?" He asks. "Brain cancer? Alzheimer's?"

She's not the best of us. She won't be allowed into Brian's grotesquely optimized future. I lean in close to one of the aquariums, as if I'm so interested by what's inside that I've forgotten to answer the question.

From behind me, I hear a wet, sucking sound. Brian grunts, maybe at me or maybe at whatever made the noise. "Okay, don't tell me. She's got you trained pretty good, hasn't she?" In the space between sentences, his voice sharpens. Becomes nastier. "If you want my advice, I'd say, remember that it's natural to leave the weak behind."

I won't let him see the wrath that kicks up in me. I won't let him know the betrayal like poison in my veins. I will smile and nod and pretend along because I need him. I will. I can do that. I can. No, I can't.

"I'm not going to abandon my family." As soon as it's out, I shut my mouth tight and try to make myself want to take it back. But like before, he doesn't really seem to care.

"There you go, talking like Bill. Well, whatever you say. All I think is, it's about time we get real about what we are. I'm not the only one who thinks so." He hesitates, like he's considering saying something more, then changes his mind. His fingers caress the edges of the nearest aquarium. “It’s a good time, talking to your uncle about lab stuff. There aren’t many people who know equipment like he does.”

As I’m saying a silent thank-you for the change of subject, something clicks into place. Now that I’m looking for it, the signs are everywhere: UNLV decals on a few of the tanks, long since colored over in black Sharpie, remnants of scraped-off barcode stickers and sanded-down serial numbers on some of the larger equipment.

“He got you all this stuff,” I breathe.

Brian shrugs. “Like I said, he’s a good guy. I’m helping you out because I owe him one.”

I notice the present tense. I notice, too, the debt. Maybe that’s all we are, in the end, a series of ever-deepening obligations owed to family we know we need but aren’t sure if we like. The other carnage is ancillary.

Brian hauls one of the aquariums off the shelf, onto the sterile slab of island in the center of the room. “Now, we need that cooler.”

18

SUNBAKED PAINT SINGES MY PALMS AS I SLAM THE trunk of Veer's car closed. I try not to wince. I didn't wince when Brian extracted vial after vial from the lumps of tissue in his basement lab. I helped him pack it in ice and hauled the cooler up the stairs balanced on my shoulder. I didn't want him to carry it for me.

"Thanks," I mumble, then clear my throat. Keep it polite. "I really appreciate it. I'll try not to bother you again."

"No problem." Brian shrugs, squinting into the sun from under his baseball cap. "Just don't make a habit of it. And don't tell your mom how to find me."

"Yeah. Even if I did, she . . ." I catch myself before I finish the sentence with *wouldn't remember it anyway.* "I won't."

"Anything I can get you for the road?"

I think of the orangey, stinking water. "No thanks."

"Okay." He scratches his arm. His nails run red tracks through the dark hair. "It's a long drive back. You can think about what I said."

I dig my thumb into the key fob, and the car warbles its response. I don't have to entertain Brian's delusions of supremacy. He doesn't know what's real any more than I do.

"Actually." I pause with the car door halfway open, my hip wedged into the space it makes. "Did Uncle Bill ever mention a woman named Martina to you? A friend of his, maybe?"

"Don't think so."

"She disappeared last year?"

"Doesn't ring a bell."

Last try. "Okay, did he ever say anything weird about, like, flayed men? I texted you about it, but I wasn't sure . . ."

Brian turns. His shadow falls across me. He looks bigger, suddenly, from this angle.

"Where I grew up, we called him 'the man from the desert,'" he says softly. "But he's a story someone made up to scare kids. That's all."

"No, yeah, I know." Something in his tone makes me want to get into the driver's seat and push the gas pedal as far down as it goes. "It's just, I don't know. When I went to check on Uncle Bill's house, it looked like someone had broken into his office, and he'd been writing an email to someone about the flayed man—the man from the desert. I thought maybe it was you."

Brian lifts his ball cap to run a sweaty hand over his forehead, then shoves the cap back over his eyes. "And?"

"My mom's been talking about him too. Claiming she saw him."

Those ice-chip eyes fix on me. "Maybe she did see him."

"You just said he's made up."

The muscle under one of his eyes twitches. "I know what I said."

"Anyway, our version doesn't live in the desert."

"Maybe there are two of them."

I'm not sure what to say to that.

Brian looks straight into the wind and says, still in that same soft voice, "Well, since you're so interested, here's how we tell it out here. A long time ago, there were more of us, a lot more, and we wandered the deserts of the world. Mojave, Atacama, Gobi. His people, our ancestors, they didn't try to hide. They weren't afraid to kill."

The wind howls, and I taste sulfur.

"Their one rule was 'We stick together.' We kill them, not each other. But the man from the desert, he was ambitious. And he was smart. He knew that he could live without limits, if he wasn't afraid to break the rules."

It's different from the version I know, but I can guess what comes next. "He turned on his family," I whisper. "He ate their hearts, so he could live forever."

"Something like that." Brian's smile is ghoulish. "He hunted the weak willed first, the ones who trailed too far behind. And he hunted the ones who challenged him, who tried to claim that solidarity or assimilation were the key to freedom. And then, eventually, he began to hunt for fun. Now, what we tell kids out here, is that he's still out there, waiting in the canyons. He lures you in by claiming he can tell the future, but if you see him, you'd better not stick around to listen. You'd better run. Because once you see him, that means he's got your scent. That means he's coming to eat your heart."

My own chest spasms, muscle and iron and bone.

"He's got no human suit, so he can only hunt at night," he continues. The wind dies down, and for a second, the world is all yellow light. "But he's got a thousand years of practice."

I blink, and there's Brian, and the brown of the house and the brown of the desert.

"But it's all bullshit, right? My mom just, she keeps talking about him like . . ."

Brian leans in. The desert air slides slimy fingers up my back. "Bill thought it was real. How about when he gets back, you ask him."

I smell his mixture of sweat and mistrust, antibacterial spray and a lifetime of believing in his own superiority. I smell his curse rearing on its hind legs, desperate to attack. And him, deciding whether to loose the chain.

"Are you fucking with me, Bill's niece?" he whispers.

"No," I choke out. "Sorry—it's really not—thanks for helping us out."

Then the moment's gone. No more dread. No more threat blocking out the sun.

"Sure." Brian reaches around me to tug the car door fully open. It's like the last few minutes, the conversation about the flayed man, never happened. "Anytime."

I smile big enough to show my back teeth and say, "Appreciate it."

As I settle into the driver's seat, Brian calls, "Hey." He retraces the path from his door to my car. Something metal jingles in one of his pockets. "Give me your email."

I find myself frozen. Prey again.

Brian scowls. "Or not."

"No, um." I scramble for a smile. This is a sign that Brian wants to keep helping us, right? I spell out my email address, waiting for him to type it into his phone or write it down on a notepad, but he just nods.

"Okay. Drive safe now." And he's disappeared back through the brown door and into the brown house, the only sign of him the faint movement of one of the curtains.

My back twinges as I pull away from the curb. I can't get myself to relax, even with Brian out of sight. The steering wheel is so hot to the touch I'm scared to breathe in, in case I smell my palms burning. A rusty kid's bike lies abandoned in the driveway next door. I wonder again about Brian's neighbors.

Better not to.

It takes me till I get back on the highway to finally fill my lungs all the way. What's in the trunk will feed us for two weeks. That's two more weeks to find another solution, because I'm sure as hell not coming back here.

I don't think to check my phone until twenty minutes into the drive. There are three texts from Veer.

Twenty-three minutes ago: *All done*

Eighteen minutes ago: *Ellis? You okay?*

Six minutes ago: *where are you. please come back already I hate this place fuck*

Sorry, I text back. *Be there in ten*

When I pull up, she's squatting on the curb, elbows on knees, face a hurricane.

"It was fine," she growls, before I can ask. "Let's get out of here."

As the highway unfurls under our tires, the sky grows dull and dark, the color of a fresh bruise. Veer is restless in the driver's seat, putting on music, then turning it down, alternating between humming to herself and squinting into the windshield. When we stop for gas and fresh ice, I text Joanne: *Have you been able to check on my mom today? How is she?*

Yesterday the desert was so beautiful. Now it's just gray blankness.

It starts to drizzle as the stoplights fade and we cross into another long, dead stretch of asphalt. We sit in silence. What's waiting for me at home? Rage? Hurt? Desolation? Or what if, worse, she woke up again while I was gone, brain fully functional, memory patched over, and I wasn't there to hold it tight and make it last?

I told her I hated her.

I told her I hated her, and then I left.

Veer coughs. I can smell everything—her reticence, her longing, her fear that she's fucked this all up. She hasn't, of course. It was me.

"So." Her fingers drum on the steering wheel. "Seen anything good lately?"

"Not really." I watch thirty-year-old sitcoms because sometimes that's the only thing that keeps my mom from breaking down in tears. I haven't seen anything new in months. "You?"

"That movie about a bunch of farmers in a murder cult. Did you see it?"

"No."

"It was terrible. Like, really bad." She laughs, and for a second the fog lifts and I feel like myself again. "Not even, like, so bad it's good. Just, straight up, sucks that I wasted my money on a movie ticket, bad, bad, bad."

She goes for another laugh, but it comes out strained. I'm not sure what to say.

"Does your mom like movies?" she asks, after a while.

"No."

"Does your uncle?"

"I don't know."

"Okay. Do you have any plans this weekend?"

"No." I want to cry. I want to say something true. I can't seem to do either. "Just work."

She gives me a look and doesn't try again.

The rain starts up as we cross back through Tonopah. Big fat drops, beating down on the windshield like drumbeats. Veer smacks the windshield wipers awake. We haven't said a word to each other in forty-five minutes.

Veer brakes too hard at the red light. My seat belt bites in my shoulder.

"Mother*fucker*," she spits.

She slaps the wheel with the butt of her palm, cutting through the background noise of rain and rubber on asphalt like a gunshot.

"So, what did I do to piss you off?" Rage simmers just below her words.

"Nothing." She's read me all wrong. I'm not pissed off, I'm knotted up. I'm a clogged drain, I'm a dead end.

"Bullshit. You've been weird ever since you picked me up. Do you have a problem with me? Is my shit, I don't know, too shitty for you?"

"No." I try to find the right words. They all seem to come to me at the wrong angles. "I had a . . ." A conversation I didn't want. A debt I don't need. One more person trying to convince me my mom isn't worth caring about. "I had a weird encounter. With a friend of my uncle's."

"Well, I had a weird fucking encounter too. With my goddamn brother. Ever consider that?" She grabs my wrist and pulls it toward her, shaking me like a dog shakes a small animal it's caught. "And by the way, I didn't have to. Nobody's forcing me to see him, it's not like I owe him a visit. I don't owe him shit."

My pulse flutters against her grip. Debts are supposed to be repaid, aren't they?

"Right, Ellis?"

"Right," I mumble.

The light turns green. Cars jerk forward.

We rumble past a teenage girl perched lonesome on the curb of an empty driveway, swallowed up by a sweatshirt with its hood up. I remember Veer folded onto the prison curb, her sharpest parts unsheathed.

"Tell me," I say.

A long second, her nails nipping my wrist. I feel her weigh her options: Throw my hand away. Snap my bones in two. Open the car door and hurl me into the roiling ocean of pavement at sixty miles per hour.

Her shoulders slump. She relaxes her grip on me, sits back, eases off the gas.

"I love him, I really do," she says. Starting quiet, but her voice grows in intensity as she continues. "And I care about him a lot. I wanted to visit him, I came up because I wanted to, because I want this relationship with him. But it's this shitty thing, where I feel like there's so much I want to forgive him for, for not being there, for doing some really fucked-up stuff when I was in high school, because once I forgive him, I'll forgive myself too. But then I see him and it's, like, all he wants is forgiveness. Or, like, not real forgiveness, he just wants me to say, 'I forgive you.' He wants me to reassure him. So I spend all my time telling him it's okay, I still love him, and there's no room for me to say, 'It's complicated. I'm angry. And that's okay, I'm here and I'm going to keep coming back, but I'm also really hurt. You made my life really hard in a lot of ways.' But there's no way to get him to understand that, no way that doesn't end with me having to do all these emotional contortions to swear to him I don't resent him." She sucks in a breath. "Which only makes me resent him more."

I turn my eyes to the rivulets of rain threading fat fingers across the window. I know how that feels. I've felt it too, but I learned to call it failure.

"I just wish it didn't still bother me," she continues. "I know it's a sign of progress that I know that's what's happening, but knowing doesn't make me feel like less of a piece of shit." Her fingers drum on the steering wheel. "I'm not taking it out on myself anymore, you know, cutting, putting cigarettes out on my arm, acting like nothing hurts me. Or like nothing can hurt me more than I can hurt myself. But sometimes I feel like that was easier."

So this is what Veer meant when she said that there was poison in her blood. She meant that she isn't afraid of pain, she's afraid of pity. If someone hurts her, she'd rather join them in carving off pieces of herself so when anyone asks, *Who did this to you*, she can say, *I did.*

"I'm not a bad person," Veer mutters. She fiddles with the windshield wiper control. Looking directly at her feels invasive, or maybe just too intimate, so I look past her at the rain drawing tear tracks through the dust on the window.

"I know."

"No, you don't." The words are a slap on my outstretched palms. "You, like, barely know me."

I glance at the GPS display on her phone. A few more hours until we're back to Vegas.

"That's true," I say. "But I'd like to know you better."

She's quiet as we sit at a red light, dwarfed by the pickup in front of us with a bumper sticker showing two stick parents, two kids, and a curly-tailed dog. Just before the light turns, she whispers, "Why?"

"I like how you look at me like there's nothing else to see." Focus on the water droplets sliding down the windshield, not on the tightness around her eyes. Not on the clutch of her fingers around the steering wheel. "I feel good when I'm with you."

The smell of the air shifts. Shit coffee and recycled air give way to a smell like a dry lake before a storm.

"And," I finish awkwardly, "you're, like, incredibly hot."

Veer laughs. The tense lines about her eyes soften. "Damn right I am."

She slips her fingers around mine, lifts my hand to her mouth at the next red light and holds it there as the highway opens up again. The monotone gray of the sky shifts a shade brighter.

"It's a whole other world out there," Veer whispers, her lips tracing my knuckles, her eyes on the craters of rock and sand and Joshua trees. "Makes you hopeful, doesn't it?"

I roll down the window to smell the musk of the rain-kissed desert, to feel the pressure in my ears, to remind myself that this is all real.

Maybe. And again, out loud. "Maybe."

Then, too soon, we're turning into my apartment building, and it's over.

"Hey." Veer pops the trunk with a noise like a pneumonia cough. "Let me help you carry your stuff."

"It's okay, I've got it." I force myself out of the passenger seat, sling the duffel bag over my shoulder, and haul the cooler out of the back. The trunk booms shut to reveal Veer, hands in pockets, waiting for me. She smiles with half her mouth and pulls the cooler out of my hands before I can protest.

"Seriously," she says. "You don't want to ruin your mom's stuff right outside the apartment, do you?"

On the drive, I told her it was some homeopathic stuff that calms my mom down. She kind of stuck her tongue out at that, but didn't argue.

She's right, though. I worked hard for that blood, and I can't replace it. So I let her heft it under her armpit and follow me up the stairs. It'll be fine. My mom might be in her bedroom or doing her hair. She might not even notice. If she does, she'll forget it sooner or later. Probably sooner.

And, selfishly, I don't want to say goodbye just yet. Let it last just a little longer. Let it stay with us as we climb the stairs, as I stamp my sneakers over the welcome mat, as I fiddle with my key and notice Veer's eyes scanning the run-down flooring and the identical rows of forest-green doors. What does she think about me, knowing this is how I live?

It doesn't matter, I remind myself, and take a deep breath as I push through the door.

And smell blood.

19

MY EYES ADJUST TOO SLOW. RED PLASTIC CUP AND RED stains on peeling gray linoleum and Veer's fast intake of breath. Everything smells wrong, like the emergency department at the end of a long night.

The cup comes into focus first, rolling in a disconsolate half circle, painting a windshield wiper arc of red. Then comes the withered legs encased in thick socks. One clog still on, the other somewhere in the shadows. The air is thick with the protein richness of crushed cartilage and the iron panic of injury.

Then all of it comes at once.

Joanne on her back on the kitchen floor, barely moving, gray hair spilling across the linoleum. My mom straddling her, mouth smeared with blood. Not the mixture of blood and vitamin C and water that's forming a puddle on the floor near Joanne's hand. Just blood.

Joanne's blood.

"Holy shit," Veer breathes, and then she's pushed the

cooler back into my arms and she's moving, and I need to be moving too.

I'm still with it enough to shove the cooler onto the counter before I rush up behind my mom, hands under her armpits, haul her away. Barely. I'm terrified of her and myself and of looking down at Joanne and seeing just what's been done to her. My mom writhes in my arms. Her bones shift under her skin.

"Call 911," Veer barks. "First aid kit."

She's on her knees next to Joanne, checking her airway. My mom howls, guttural and furious. The back of her head clips my chin.

First aid kit.

I keep one arm around my mom and lunge for the cupboard under the sink. Right next to our sharps container. My arm erupts in pinpricks of pain. My mom's dragged her fingernails down the length of it. No, not fingernails. Claws. Her hands are grotesque, one moment huge and menacing as the animal inside gains the upper hand, the next collapsing back into a fistful of withered fingers. She's an old woman. She's so strong. She's screaming, or maybe I'm screaming. Maybe both.

"Under the sink," I shout to Veer, and hope that's enough. I need both hands and all my strength to keep hold of my mom. Her screaming mouth turns snoutlike and dripping, curved fangs sickling out of her gums, and I catch her by the neck just in time to stop her from taking a bite out of my arm.

Then I see her eyes.

Their gray depths are formless and terrified. Tears streak down her cheeks as the planes of her face shift and warp.

How can I blame her for what she's done?

She howls again, claws erupting from her fingers, reaching for my face this time. I shove her into the bathroom and slam the door and expect her to come for me, to start battering her way through it, but it goes quiet inside.

I call 911 with slick fingers and sprint back to the kitchen for a vial from the cooler. If she attacked Joanne, it means she's hungry. The first aid kit is scattered around Veer. She's pulled her shirt off, pressing it to Joanne's neck, speaking low and quiet.

"Stay with me," I hear, and then her voice goes loud and commanding. "She good?"

No, my mom isn't good. She hasn't been good and she never will be, and I can't say that now, because there's a woman dying on my kitchen floor and Veer is the only reason she might make it to the hospital.

"Got her in the bathroom," I tell her, which is the best I can do.

"Good."

The dispatcher cuts in from my phone, crisp and unhurried. "911, what's your location?"

I rap out the address as I stumble back to the bathroom. "My neighbor is here, she has some kind of neck injury. Level I. She's bleeding a lot."

"Can you describe what happened?"

"I don't know. I just got back from out of town and she was . . ."

I don't know how to finish the sentence. He assures me an ambulance is already on its way.

I find my mom crouched against the toilet, a shrunken

version of herself with frenzied eyes, her exposed arms draped in a grotesque quilt of scratches. Saliva froths over her lower lip, adding pinkish bubbles to the blood still streaking her chin. But she's not transforming anymore. She's gotten enough control back.

"What's happening?" she whispers. Her eyes are wide, terrified. "Is everything okay?"

I can't tell her. I'm not going to tell her.

I rip a disposable syringe from its plastic sheath. "Give me your arm."

She shrinks back, her frail arms wrapping reflexively around herself. My mouth goes ashy.

"Hey, Mom, it's me." I try to soften my voice, paste a smile on my face, tense my lips to keep my teeth covered. "I know you're hungry. I just want to help."

She nods, but when she extends her arm to me, it's shaking.

I fill the syringe. "Make a fist for me."

She obeys, hand nestled in my lap. The fist flops open as the barrel empties, her shoulders softening, cuts fluttering like flower petals as they begin to knit back together.

For a second, reality softens too. Maybe I've fallen asleep to the sound of the rain on Veer's windshield and this is a nightmare I'll jolt awake from, sweaty and thankful.

The door slams open hard enough to bounce off the wall.

"Ambulance is here," Veer barks. "Want help with her?"

She's silhouetted in the doorway, red spattering her sports bra. My mom cowers at the sight of her.

"I'll drive her later," I lie. Hospitals aren't good for creatures like us. "She's still calming down."

"'Kay." Veer frowns, begins to backtrack. Her eyes catch on the needle still in my hand.

I go to hide it automatically, then think better of it. "It's not—"

"What it looks like. Yeah." For a second, her face spasms like she's on the verge of tears. "Is it ever?"

I start to stand, but my mom's hand grabs me and squeezes. I can't. She needs me.

By the time I turn back to the doorway, it's empty, the door still swinging restless on its hinges.

I push it closed, my stomach knotted, and squeeze my mom's hand in reply. Her eyes drift closed. I watch as tears bloom from beneath her eyelids and race each other down her cheeks.

"Me and you, Mom," I whisper to her. "It's just me and you."

When the medics' voices fade and the front door slams for the last time, I still wait ten minutes before venturing back into the kitchen. Boots and bodies have smeared crimson tracks across the floor. The scent of it nudges my curse awake, a hungry purr deep in its throat. When I run the faucet, the water that comes out in demanding spurts stinks like formaldehyde.

Veer is gone. I knew she would be, packed in the ambulance with the medics—her people, safe people—but I still feel bereft, pacing the room without her. I stack the vials from the cooler in the freezer, safe and secure this time. It takes three rags to mop up all the blood on the floor. Once I've changed into clean clothes and scrubbed any residual spatter off my arms, I toss the rags in a plastic grocery bag and take them out to the dumpster.

Horror, I remind myself as I try to brand the image of Joanne's collapsed body into my brain. I should be feeling horror.

She was good to us. Well, as good as could be expected. Did she recoil when my mom went for her throat, or did it happen so fast that she didn't even know to react?

The dumpster slams shut, almost catching my fingers. Horror. But it's just a word, not a real feeling. Here is what I actually feel: relief. It could have been so much worse. It's too easy to imagine—Veer opening the door, cooler in hand, met with hunger moving too fast for me to stop. Or if we'd lingered at the gas station a few minutes longer and come back to find my mom already lost to me, no way to put her down but death. No, it was only Joanne.

What a thing to think. I'm the one with poison in my blood, not Veer.

Veer, with her bruised knees and her smell like citrus soap and longing. What, exactly, did she see? Joanne's sprawled frame and ruined neck, sure, but how much else?

I don't want to know. Any of it, all of it, is too much.

On my way back to the apartment, I pass another neighbor in the stairwell. A young mother and her preteen daughter, her hair in two long braids tied with gold ribbons.

"Was that the police here just now?" the mother asks. She grips a vase of fresh lilies. Her other hand is holding her daughter's.

"I think it was an ambulance."

She looks concerned. "Ambulance? Did someone have an accident?"

"I'm not sure."

"Oh." The daughter winces. I imagine her mother's grip tightening, a handcuff she can't unlock. "I hope everything's okay."

"Yeah. Me too."

As they continue down the stairs, the daughter glances back at me, like she knows.

We can't stay here. After ambulances come law enforcement, and after that come too many questions we can't answer. The surest way to survive is to leave first. Just the two of us against the world. Just me and my mom's failing mind.

Tears prick at the back of my throat. I thought I hated Vegas, thought I hated the neon Post-its and my teenage bedspread. It's been a shit life, but it's been mine. Ours, mine and my mom's. But what's my life been but an exercise in sorting out what matters, and learning to abandon the rest?

I don't even consider the possibility that my mom's killed someone. What that might mean for the odds of them coming after us, what that might mean if we're caught, how that might change things between us. It's one of the things that doesn't matter. Better to hit the road and keep going until we can't anymore.

Maybe Arizona. I've never been to Arizona.

Back in the bathroom, my mom is still huddled against the toilet, eyes half-closed. Dispatch probably already put a call through to LVMPD. They'll be on the way soon, full of a different, worse kind of hunger than ours. I explain it all to my mom, what's coming and what we have to do before it gets here, but I'm not sure she hears me.

"I want to take a bath," she mumbles. Her voice is syrupy.

She says it like she needs this, and I don't have it in me to deny her one last luxury before we return to our old life, our sad, lonely road life.

"Okay." I step over her and reach for the faucet. Hot water slops over my fingers. "It'll be ready in a few minutes. I'll pack our bags while you're in."

When I was little, when we had the luxury of a bathtub in whatever month-to-month place my mom got, she'd run me a bath every Sunday. Bubble bath and everything, and she'd perch on the side of the tub and wash my hair as I babbled about school and friends and whatever else it is kids get excited about. Those were good times. At least, at first. Then we stayed too long in Colorado, and her fingers grew possessive on my scalp.

"How was school?" she'd demand. "Who are your friends? What do their parents do?" Nails biting into the skin behind my ears. "Do you like them more than me? Would you rather I never existed?" And I'd thrust my inadequate hands into hers, swearing over and over again I loved her best.

"I know," she'd relent, eventually. "You're my angel. No one understands me like you do, Ellis."

"And," she'd add, eyes glassy with warning, "no one ever will."

As her bloody clothes pool on the bath mat, I murmur, "Let me wash your hair, Mom."

Maybe it's a plea for forgiveness. Maybe I want to remind her where we started. Maybe I want to remind myself that we've done this before, and that we can do it again.

Maybe it doesn't matter why. Just that I want to do it for her, and she lets me.

I massage the shampoo into a lavender-scented slick in my hands. Her hair is getting thinner. She's thinner too, skin folding around birdlike bones that look like they're one bad fall away from snapping. Her joints are purple and swollen, small cuts like wailing mouths kaleidoscoping out around each one.

"What happened, Mom?" I try to say it softly.

She sighs, eyes closed, and my heart sinks, thinking that's all the answer I'll get. Then, hoarsely: "He came."

"Who came?" I ask automatically. But I already know. I drop my voice to a whisper. "The flayed man."

She grunts assent. "He's going to eat me alive."

"I won't let that happen."

Her smile is a fault line. "You don't have a choice. He's coming."

She's only saying it because she lost control, because the story goes that once you transform, even for an instant, he'll catch your scent. But Brian didn't mention that in his version, and anyway, she just feels guilty. She knows, somewhere, that all of this is her fault. At least, that's what I tell myself. I don't have time for fear. I have an apartment to pack up.

I grab my mom's hand out of the soapy water and squeeze hard. "Feel that?"

She nods. Her skin radiates warmth from the hot water. Her fingers squeeze me back.

"I'm here. Is the flayed man here?"

Her smile cracks at the edges, and she shakes her head.

"That's right. I'm real, and he's not." I take a deep breath through my nose. If I breathe through my mouth, my voice will shake. "I've got you."

I don't care if it's a lie.

20

I GIVE MY MOM A FEW MINUTES TO SOAK IN PEACE, then rinse her hair out and leave the showerhead dangling impotently over the side of the tub. There's nothing remarkable about the way the soapy water ebbs around her sagging frame, or the shaky way she climbs out. How could I hate someone so feeble? How could I blame her for everything she's done?

Then I remember the scent of Joanne's blood, like congealed oatmeal and plastic flowers and fingers stained green from latching and unlatching the door chain.

My mom shuffles to her bedroom and begins pulling on her pajamas.

"I started packing for you," I explain, gesturing at the suitcase splayed open on the floor like a pinned butterfly. Her favorite sandals nestle against rolled-up sweaters, wispy blouses, the entire contents of her underwear drawer. "What else do you want to bring?"

She turns her back on it all. Tugs at the pink-and-cream florals of her sheets.

"I'm tired," she murmurs as she crawls into bed.

"No, Mom, we have to go."

Her hair splays across the pillowcase. "You're so dramatic."

"No, I'm not, can we please—" I swallow the rest of what I want to say. There's no time for bargaining, even less for an argument. "You can nap while I finish packing and get the car. I'll wake you up as soon as I'm done, and then we're leaving. Okay?"

She sinks into the floral embrace of her silky pillows and ignores me. Is this what it's going to be like, for the rest of time?

As I turn to go, my mom stirs. "Ellis, baby."

"Yeah?"

Her voice sounds like melted Jolly Ranchers, strange-sweet and syrupy. "Remember that time when you left your math homework behind at that gas station? Where was that?"

"Grand Junction," I mutter. "And it was a rest stop."

Her laugh flutters like wind chimes, and she pushes a damp chunk of hair back from her forehead. "Yeah. And we drove three extra hours back through the mountains to get it, remember?"

I remember, Mom. And I remember every goddamn time you've reminded me of it.

I already know what comes next. Except it doesn't. Instead, she sighs, "The desert was so beautiful that day."

My stomach clenches. I forgot that part. The sky so blue and cloudless it was like a child's drawing, the orange-red mesas slipping by, crowned with towering rocks like winking monuments that whispered, *Everything changes, if you just wait long enough.* Scrubby trees the color of burnt coffee and tumbleweeds like hungry bundles of razor wire and the endlessness that took my breath away, that made me feel blissfully inconsequential, like I could do anything and the world would let me.

That was the first time I fell in love with the desert. In the tug-of-war my mom's disease set us on, I'd forgotten all about the wonder of it.

"It was, Mom," I say, my throat thick. "It really was."

Her eyes flutter closed, and her breathing slips into a soft, even rhythm.

When I was a kid, the nights I couldn't sleep I'd shuffle my way to my mom's bed, a glass of orange juice or a slice of buttered toast in hand as an offering, and she'd mumble awake and let me curl up on top of the duvet like a cat. I'd wake there in the morning with a discarded plate or a dusting of crumbs next to my head and study my mom as she slept: the careful way her cuticles were pushed back to make way for her nail polish, the silk daintiness of her pillows and the way sleep made her breath ragged and rhythmic. In those moments, perfection felt just out of reach. Another minute, and I'd know who I was supposed to be. Always, just before I found out, her alarm would blare or she'd roll over and snort awake. Maybe next time, I'd tell myself. I just have to keep trying.

If I nestled on top of the covers with her now, would it feel the same? Would I finally catch that thing that will remake me the way my mom wants?

A vibration in my pocket. I pull out my phone, and Veer's name sears my vision.

For a second, I consider declining her call. Let it go back to me and my mom, like old times. Except if I lie down, I might fall asleep, and I have to be the adult here. I have to get us ready to run.

When I press the phone to my ear, I find my throat's dried up and I can't bring myself to speak. There's a long, heavy pause before Veer says, "Ellis?"

"Yeah." The word scratches my throat on the way out.

"I thought I should call. Um, how are you holding up?"

The fuzziness of the connection can't hide the exhaustion in her voice.

"My mom's asleep."

"I didn't ask about her."

I tiptoe through the kitchen and slip out the front door. What am I supposed to tell her? That my body is bloodthirsty and my mom's a monster? That we're preparing to skip town without saying goodbye? That I'm beaten down and overwhelmed and it's taking all my strength to hold back the flood of terror waiting to break over me if I take even a moment to think about what might happen to us?

"Is Joanne okay?" I ask, instead of answering.

I can hear Veer's swallow on the other end of the line. "We worked her all the way there, but, you know. She'd lost a lot of blood."

I don't want to hear the thing that Veer is trying not to say, but, like a scab I can't stop picking at, I'm also desperate to make her say it.

"But you got her to the hospital," I prod.

"We worked her all the way there, Ellis." She says my name like a diagnosis. "Because I care about my fucking job. We both know it didn't make a difference."

I want to feel guilty. I want to feel monstrous. Instead, I feel nothing.

"Okay," I say, numbly.

"The cops will want to talk to your mom."

A strangled feeling pinches my throat. "You talked to the police?"

"She died, Ellis," Veer snarls.

"What did you tell them?"

"I don't know." Agitation makes her words come faster. "That there was a lot of blood. I don't know what happened."

She could have told them about my mom's warping jaws, and the needle she saw in my hand. But she didn't. I don't want her pity. I can't be in debt to Veer, not now.

"Why'd you tell them that?" I snap. It sounds like an accusation.

"Because I don't know what I saw!" I can't help my flinch. Her rage is palpable, even through the phone. "So you'd better figure out what you want to say, because otherwise they're going to figure it out for you."

A small silence. She's waiting on my answer.

"Thanks, I guess." I hate how lifeless it sounds.

"Okay, then." Her voice turns sharp edged, almost cruel. "Don't say I didn't warn you."

I realize, too late, that it's not pity she's offering after all. Not even protection. It's the power to decide for myself what comes next.

I want to reach out and take it. But she's already hung up.

That stings. But there's still my suitcase, and the car, and the waiting road.

Except when I let myself back into the apartment, something smells off. I'm reminded of the house party and the eaves that wept blood, and of the sticky, congealed darkness around the edges of Uncle Bill's freezer. Of the arid desert aroma in his office.

That's what the air smells like now.

A twinge behind my belly button. I fumble for the dead bolt, but my hands land six inches to the left of where they should. The shadows are too dark, the space around them too bright. I shut my eyes to reorient myself, but it plunges me into a cacophony of scent: dry flesh stretched to breaking, bones picked clean by wind.

I think I open my eyes, but all I see is blankness. I try to blink a few times. Nothing changes. Are my eyes still closed? Are my feet still on the ground? I'm suspended in the void, I've fallen down a well.

No, I'm in our apartment. My mom is in the bedroom. I'm in shock, or I'm having a seizure, or who knows what the fuck else, but I know one thing: none of this is real.

My eyes are still closed. I just have to open them.

When I do, all I see is yellow.

Dazzling yellow light streams from everywhere and nowhere. Bright as the desert at noon, so bright my teeth ache. The light seeps into my ears, sets them buzzing, then ringing, then pounding until I'm sure there's blood pouring from them. I can't move my arms to check. They don't listen to me anymore. Maybe they're not even there.

A shape emerges from the glare. Two arms, two legs, one head, but it smells like roadkill and stagnant water. Like vinegar and sludgy flesh, like rotting planks in the aftermath of a house fire. It drags itself forward on segmented legs, knees bent backward, shoulders pinned together like the haunches of a four-legged predator. Its rib cage is flayed open to reveal a blighted chasm shivering with maggots. Terror blooms in my joints, in the hollow of my chest where my curse lies in wait, ready to flay my torso open in the same way if I let it. The animal inside me growls low and dangerous and presses itself against the bars of its cage, and I know who he is without needing to know why.

The flayed man lurches closer, and his face jolts into focus against the bright yellow invading my skull. A face eaten down to the bone, long white worms coiling between sagging layers of decayed muscle and graying fat. He draws a rattling breath. The worms of his face shiver in place and then, in a single sinuous movement, flow into the yawning oval darkness of his mouth.

My vision fills with slurred images. Clouds' shadows as they drift over cracked earth. The nightly path of the constellations. Trucks drawing trails of light down the highway.

I've been watching you.

They're not words, and I don't hear them. One minute my head is full of pictures and the next they're gone and only the impression of the words remains. Is this how my mom feels, when nothing makes sense? I want to spit in his face. I want to attack. I want to do something, anything, but my body has deserted me.

The flayed man shakes his head. Maggots tumble over his lower lip.

Restraint is tedious, don't you think? This time, the images are of carrion, of discarded protein bar wrappers spinning away on the wind. *Why not give in?*

Temptation smells like spent matches and sugar. I could let go and be consumed by the beast roaming restless in my chest. How would it feel? Agonizing. Sublime. My throat spasms, and I suddenly have control of my tongue. "My mom—"

His face doesn't move, but my mind is filled with his laugh. An earthquake, an avalanche, rattling my skull, shaking me by the neck like a predator.

You'll see. Hunting is sweetest with a pack.

He pivots on broken legs, graying tendons stretching to their breaking point. The yellow light grows brighter, making him shimmer like a mirage.

Run, if you like. But running is for prey. Are you prey?

An urgent beat against my ribs. I need to say something, to ask him, to demand—

The flayed man turns back to me, and his eyes glitter like twin abysses as he opens his mouth and howls.

A keratin shiver the length of my limbs. Not a sound, but an aftermath of sound, a reverberation that shoves like cactus spines against my eardrums. My curse bolts, chain rippling loose and molten, as the flayed man howls again and the yellow becomes even brighter, so bright it pierces my eyeballs and shreds the nerves beyond. My palms burn and my knuckles crack and, for a second, the chain wraps around my ankles and I'm not sure of my hands and my joints wail their desire to twist into something monstrous.

Iron in my hands. Don't think, just control. My breath is hot and fast, but the chain is there. When I pull, it coats my face with tears that taste like ash. Inch by inch, I haul my hunger back into its cage. When I open my eyes, the yellow light is gone and the flayed man is gone too. I'm curled on my side on the linoleum, my tongue caustic with rotten cactus and grief, I'm a canyon in a flash flood and I'm drowning, and then it's gone and it's only me and the kitchen floor and the sudden horror of returning to what's real.

My heartbeat presses furiously into my windpipe. My knuckles are purple and misshapen, my wrists splintered and useless. I shut my eyes and the yellow aftermath lingers.

Just pretend it's not real, Ellis. Pretend it's just one more thing to outrun. But I can't, it's already in my brain, terror riding the wave of nausea rising through me. The flayed man is real, and he howled out my curse and left me at its mercy.

My throat spasms. I cough, and it becomes a dry heave, and my ears are ringing again, and fear is ripping through my stomach. Once you see him, he's got your scent. That's what Brian said. Once you see him, he's coming to eat your heart.

I need to tell my mom that I believe her, that I know why she attacked Joanne, that he tried it on me too. I need to get up. My limbs feel too light, like they're not mine anymore. I flex my toes, just to be sure. They move when I tell them to. Come on, Ellis, get up. Get up, Ellis. Get up, get up, *get up*—

In a second. One more heartbeat to see if I can pretend it's not real. One more. One more. One more. One more. Please.

The linoleum is cool on my cheek. I wrap my arms around my knees, hug them to my torso. The flayed man is gone. He can't touch me. Just as soon as I get my breathing steady, I'll get up, I'll check on my mom. I'll keep the panic out of my voice, I'll reassure her, I'll do whatever it takes.

It's still there, the smell. Like a meal left out too long on a picnic table, or a cut that's starting to get infected. A dark, sticky, stinking pool oozes into the cracks in the kitchen tile. Blood that seeped from the flayed man's withered limbs while he stood. Just like the blood that was left behind in Uncle Bill's house after he disappeared.

Terror propels me upright. My damaged wrists scream in protest, but it doesn't matter. I burst through the door of my mom's bedroom, and I'm hit with the scent of carrion. A vicious crimson stain spreads across the comforter, drowning the delicate pink flowers. A knot of segmented worms gleams pale and sickly on the pillow. In the center, where the blood pools thick and sticky, is an indent in the shape of a person.

My mom is gone.

21

I STARE AT THE PLACE WHERE MY MOM ISN'T. I STARE and stare. If someone touched a lighter to my arm, I wouldn't remember to flinch until the skin was black. I'm no longer something permanent.

Then I scream.

It tears out of my throat like an invasive vine. I gag on it, keep screaming, unable to stop long enough to breathe. I cry like I'm coughing up my lungs, harsh, racking sobs that tear at my windpipe.

My legs give out under me, and it's a relief. The sharp crack of my knees on the carpet, and the pain that radiates from them. What's the point in running if there's no one left to demand a future from me? Now that I've been robbed of my final act of love and absolution? But there's still the threat of blue-and-red lights, of heavy boots and heavier words, and more than that, there's the fact that I want to live. I still want to. I'll always want to.

So I have to run. I have to *try*.

The pink threads dangling from the hem of the comforter ripple like they're laughing. Silly girl. You tried so hard, and it meant nothing. You measured living only by what you could stand, by how thin you could stretch yourself, and none of that stopped you from being robbed of the only person who could finally say *enough*.

My vision's blurry again. She can't be gone. Not like this. Not this fast.

I don't bother with a suitcase for myself. I take the same duffel bag I brought on my road trip with Veer, with a few additions. A rain jacket. Uncle Bill's papers. Laptop. More disposable syringes and antiseptic wipes. Full-size shampoo. A Polaroid of my mom, younger, smiling, holding three-year-old me as we twirl under a wide blue-gray sky. My back is to the camera, and her eyes have the blurry look of television static, but we look happy. She looks happy.

She isn't dead. I won't believe it. A pack, the flayed man said. Maybe he's going to kill her soon, but he hasn't yet. He wants someone to hunt with first.

He'll at least keep her alive until sunrise. Once the sun's up, he needs to hide, not hunt, and he might not care to keep her around after that. Which means I have the rest of the night to find her, so I can be there with her for the end, to do my duty with a knife and gut myself on the last thing I owe her, the only way my family knows to show their devotion. I need her to forgive me.

I don't know where that thought comes from, but it's true: I need her to forgive me. For forsaking her, for resenting her, for never being enough.

The bathroom smells like lavender. Her towel is still damp. The leftover humidity runs a tongue down my cheek. I close my eyes while I pee, but all that means is I can't look at anything as a distraction.

I know so little about the flayed man. *This* flayed man. He's Brian's version, a desert dweller, not the story I grew up with.

I wash my hands, desperate to keep moving. Brian can tell me more about what he might do. Where he might go. He must know more, all that talk of eating hearts, of evolution. He took my email but didn't give me his. But I have the phone.

When I punch his contact into the Nokia, the only answer is a flat triple chirp of a disconnected line. I want to scream, but all that comes out is a sound like creaking hinges on a haunted house.

Don't think about it. Keep enduring. I have our bags and a few weeks' worth of blood. I'll get my fucked-up car, and I'll scour the state of Nevada mile by mile until I find her. Until I get my forgiveness.

In the kitchen, I smell rot.

Red on stainless steel. A trail no wider than my finger and only a little longer, trickling slowly from the bottom edge of the freezer door. I rip the freezer open, my heart in my throat.

Every single vial is smashed. The plastic grooves of the freezer bottom are soaked with blood. Slushy and slow moving, crawling its way toward me. Twisting in the glittering wreckage, the forsaken shards drawing red lines across their fat, segmented bodies, are fistfuls of the flayed man's white worms.

Hysteria claws at me. My mom fed recently, but I haven't since yesterday. I drag a finger through the pooling remnants, trying to avoid the broken glass. The smell of it makes me gag. I try not to breathe as I stick it in my mouth. Even tainted blood can sustain us, can't it?

Then I'm doubled over the sink, spitting, then heaving up

foamy pink liquid, bright spots bursting across my vision and my curse howling as if to say, *poison, poison, poison.*

The flayed man's sick blood will do nothing for my hunger.

I sob, once, and then I can't stop. I don't care if the neighbors call the cops. They're already coming. I know life isn't fair—if it was, I wouldn't have been born an abyss with teeth, but just for once, why can't it be simple? Why can't it be easy? We never had a chance. Fuck, we've never had a chance. All my life, I've been running, and I was ready to do it again, and now what?

My mouth is too dry and my throat is too raw and my eyes are swelling shut from crying. I can still smell the flayed man, faintly, the way the gritty, unwashed stink of body odor seeps around strong cologne. He caught my scent, but I caught his too. My curse's senses are sharper than mine. If I let it run, will it find him?

All I can do is reach past my lungs to where my curse snaps at its iron confines, and throw the lock.

This time, it runs with its head low and its jaws bared, arrow-sleek and single-minded. The flayed man's carrion stench fills my nose and turns my stomach. The chain goes taut, pulling me toward the highway, toward the desert, rippling agony through my bones. Pain shatters my wrists, and I wonder if this is the same pain my mom felt when the flayed man turned on her. I bite my spit-slick tongue with razor canines and imagine my skin erupting with the same flower-petal cuts that dotted her arms. Will my bruises take the same shape as hers? Pain overwhelms me, and there's no more thoughts but this: it only stops if I can stop it. And right now, I don't want to.

But years of obedience win out and I find myself curled before the wreckage of the freezer, the linoleum like ice on my overheated cheek, calm enough to think. My curse only gave me a direction, but it's a start.

Two needs scrabble urgently inside me, nipping at each other, vying for dominance: I need to find my mom. And I need to find more blood before hunger takes me apart.

I choose my mom. I always have.

I need a car.

The mechanic looks at me like I'm crazy, but he returns my keys and lets me drive away with a still-busted windshield. Maybe he smells Joanne's suffering still somewhere on my skin.

The Filipino market closes at 9:00, and I make it through the doors at 8:50. It's huge and concrete and fluorescent lit, and this time of night it's as empty as a cemetery, just me and the miserable cashiers and a solitary auntie pushing a hand truck stacked with pale slabs of frozen chicken. When she passes me in the aisle, I smell aspirin and strawberry candy and a heart drowning in fluid meant for the rest of her body.

I'm no longer a raging storm. I'm hollow. I had to press warm washcloths over my eyes to get them open enough to see properly. The Top 40 knockoff piped through the grocery store speaker warbles about late-night phone calls, and the disembodied beep of Brian's disconnected phone echoes somewhere at the back of my skull.

I find the pig's blood in the meat section at the back, packaged neatly next to shrink-wrapped lobsters and pasty sacks of uncooked fish balls. I take two containers and grab a bag of Takis and a couple of pork skewers from the hot bar to make it look more like a normal grocery run. The skewers smell good, like brown sugar and barbecue sauce. They'd smell better if they were raw.

The cashier is young, with brown lip liner and impossible lash extensions. I smell the filed-down edges of her acrylic nails, the musk she's drowned in vanilla-floral perfume. I smell bitterness and late-night diaper changes and a stomach that wishes it still knew how to fill with butterflies.

"Find everything you need?" she deadpans.

"Yeah."

"Great. $14.38." She grabs a plastic bag, and her long black ponytail catches in the silver tinsel of a miniature Christmas tree on the checkout stand. Christmas was months ago. The speakers croon something about last summer and wanting her back.

I dig in my wallet and find I have exact change. That would feel lucky, if it weren't for everything else.

Hunched in my back seat in the darkest corner of the parking lot, I suddenly miss the inane music in the grocery store. The quiet is suffocating. I pop the lid off the pig's blood, pull it into a syringe. It smells like floor cleaner and manure and an itchy not-quite-rightness, like the embarrassed prickle of calling out to someone you think is a friend but turns around to reveal a stranger. That doesn't stop it from making my mouth water and my sinuses sing.

Make a fist. Metal meets skin. Out of habit, I tense for the rush of euphoria, for the dissolving of my limbs and the soar of my heart, but it doesn't come. Just a vague weakening of the relentless beat of hunger.

It won't be enough for long.

There's always one way to get blood, if I'm willing to become a monster. There's another way too, if I'm ready to burn the last of my bridges. But not yet. My mom comes first. Finding the flayed man comes first. His scent pulled me north, into the desert, but the Mojave stretches half the state and into the next one. If I was a creature of famine and viciousness, if I burned in the daylight and stalked through the night, where would I hide? Where? I demand it of myself until the word starts to lose all meaning. Where, where, where?

And then, the question biting into me—why us?

What did we do to deserve this?

What did *I* do?

Underneath the anger, the sense of injustice, is a terror that I did this, somehow. With my ingratitude, with my disbelief. My mom was the one who ripped through Joanne's throat, but I pushed her to it, and now she's been stolen from me because I was too distracted by my girlfriend to keep watch.

Well, Veer's not my girlfriend. I like her, and we fucked once. That's not the same thing.

The truth is, there probably isn't a reason. He was just hungry, and we were closest. But maybe we weren't always. I pull up Reddit, and stare at the message I sent about Martina Revelle. *I saw her car was found near Corn Creek, but do you know exactly where?*

Martina Revelle, whose last days devolved into paranoia, who drove to the desert and ditched her car, a crime scene spattered with someone else's blood. Uncle Bill too, his car abandoned on the highway en route to Mount Charleston. Was he looking for her? I think of the way he always swallowed his words, like there were secrets he wanted to tell me but didn't dare. I remember the way Brian said so casually, "Bill thought it was real."

He wasn't looking for Martina. He was looking for the flayed man. Of all the stupid, self-absorbed—how could he?

We needed him, and he left us to play at true crime, to hunt down a monster. Don't you know that we're the monsters? Don't you know what you owe us?

Back to my phone. The poster never responded, so I send another message, just in case: *Can you help? It's urgent.*

My joints throb. For a second, I think it's from the way I'm wedged cross-legged in the back seat, but when I unfold my legs, the thrum of it only intensifies.

Hunger.

I pull out a fresh syringe and inject more pig's blood. It dampens my hunger even less this time. The insistent burn like a firmly held pinch worms its way into my gums. *MR and RV both 2017.* RV must be another person who vanished the same year, or in similar circumstances. If Uncle Bill used these disappearances to track down the flayed man, I can too.

I try searching a list of people who died or disappeared in the Las Vegas area last year, but all that turns up is an LVMPD page explaining that hundreds of people are reported missing each month, and if you want to know where someone is, try calling the jail. I try the *Review-Journal*'s crime section, but it's mostly burglaries and crooked cops. The burning sensation expands, sending shivers through my sinuses. I stretch my jaw to stop myself from clenching my teeth around nothing.

What else might be part of the pattern? Martina's supposed psychotic break? That must mean the flayed man visited her. What else? Her hiking trips? Her abandoned car? Last time I searched Mount Charleston disappearances, there was an abandoned car story too.

I search the phrase again. My hands are a little shaky, my wrists and elbows shivering in their sockets. An abandoned pickup truck, a white Chevy Silverado, found at the Mount

Charleston trailhead a couple months ago. The article's only a few paragraphs. Was there blood? Did they find out who the truck belonged to?

I try *Mt Charleston Silverado abandoned*, then *Mt Charleston abandoned truck February 2018*, and find a few more articles. The truck belonged to Craig Willard, who'd been staying with friends in Vegas for the winter but didn't seem to be from anywhere in particular. Drifter. Could be one of us. One article mentions a history of mental illness. There's no mention of blood in the truck, only that the windows were smashed. But it might have been there.

It also might not have been.

This Craig Willard isn't RV, but Mount Charleston and Corn Creek are both north of the city, on either side of Highway 95. Same direction my curse pulled me in. Same area where Uncle Bill's truck turned up, deserted, a grave marker on the side of the road. I massage my cheekbones, then pinch the bridge of my nose so hard my fingernails leave marks. The pig's blood isn't enough now, and it won't be enough to sustain me through a night of searching, and doing whatever I need to do to get my mom back from the flayed man.

I unlatch the glove compartment and reach for the Swiss Army knife I keep there for emergencies. It's not going to work, we can't drink our own blood. But do I know that for sure? It's just what my mom told me, and she lied about all sorts of things.

I press it into my forearm. The skin depresses but doesn't break. When's the last time I sharpened it? When's the last time I even thought to ask? I keep trying, and all I get is a series of dull red dents in my arm.

I brought one weapon with me. At the bottom of my duffel

bag. I push aside T-shirts and socks and ziplock-bagged toiletries as I dig for it.

Our chef's knife. Thick as my wrist, biggest one in the kitchen. I unroll the sweatshirt wrapped around it. *I've Been To Oklahoma!* it shouts in proud pink letters. One of my mom's sweatshirts that became mine as a half hand-me-down, half gift.

I cut myself with the knife meant for my mom's heart, that final thing I owe her, and press the incision to my lips. It tastes like nothing. Like less than nothing. Like tap water with too many minerals, like disappointment, like failure. I dig a Band-Aid out of the glove compartment, press it over the seam in my forearm, and bury my face in the sweatshirt. It smells like my mom. I wish that were comforting.

I want to call Veer. It was so easy, when it was just us and the road. When we sped down Highway 95, was the flayed man already watching? Was my future already carved into the lengths of his claws?

I wipe the knife on my jeans and return it to its place at the bottom of my bag. Despair thickens into a searing fog that threatens to burn my throat. I can't put my hunger off any longer.

I'm not quitting my search. I just need to do this in order to carry on.

I desperately don't want to do it.

Time to light up the last bridge left to me. There's always work for a nurse, I'll find somewhere new. I just need to survive long enough to find my mom.

I pack away the medical supplies and climb back into the driver's seat. Then I type *Sunrise Hospital* into my GPS and head for work.

22

CHANEY'S AT THE TRIAGE DESK WHEN I COME IN. I'VE changed into scrubs, better to go unnoticed around the hospital, but I still feel like everyone's staring at me.

"You're on tonight, Karsten?" Her eyes dart from side to side, appraising me.

"Covering for another floor," I lie. The sliding doors gasp open, letting in a torrent of wind and the turpentine smell of fresh asphalt.

Don't turn around. Don't hope that it's Veer. But I do, I can't help it, and the medic is a stranger who's somewhere between a linebacker and a Labrador retriever. Ying is right behind him, stone faced as always.

"Hey, Chaney," the linebacker calls as they slip on through. He looks back over his shoulder, and again I recognize the up-and-down look of inspection. Then he turns back and mutters something to Ying.

When it hits me, my stomach twists up around the rest of

my organs. Veer didn't tell me where they took Joanne, but Sunrise is our local trauma center.

I watch the medic's back until he turns the corner. I want to scream, I want to snarl, I want to curl up and disappear. I'm not a monster, you motherfucker. Neither is my mom.

I can't bring myself to look at Chaney. I rear back from the desk and head for the safety of the elevator. Hunger sets hooks into the soft flesh of my gums, and I count heartbeats in between the hollow dings of each new floor we ascend. The doors draw open like curtains before the last act.

My joints whimper. My curse salivates.

Through two doors and into a waiting room, where an older woman in flip-flops and a blue dress turns to me with a smile that asks if I've come for her. Past a window where a nurse buries her face in a computer screen, through another door and down a hall, navigating more by smell than sight.

I find an empty room and a tray of blood samples on the bottom shelf of a rolling cart. My knees lock at the smell of the samples, the sour tang of plastic tubing dissolving into iron richness. I could do it now. I could pop off the cap and pour it into my mouth.

Too late. There are already footsteps behind me.

I tuck the entire tray under my arm and start walking. I don't know where I'm headed, but in a hospital, people always pay you less attention if you're moving.

"Excuse me?" The nurse's voice is raspy. She smells like cheap jewelry and wilted spinach. "Where are you taking those?"

Deep breath. Keep moving. "I can take them down to the lab."

"The lab sent you?" She's young. She looks exhausted. I remember how that was, the terror of authority over patients, and the worse terror of having to take all the other nurses' shit and grin through it.

"Yeah. Yes." How have I bled away every instinct I had for lying?

The nurse leans in and eases the tray of samples out of my grasp. I smell espresso and aspartame. "Usually we have someone take them, not the other way around. Who sent you up here?"

I could grab one of the vials right now and clench my fist so tight it shatters. I could sink my teeth into this woman. I could tear her apart.

"Let me just call down and check." She squints at the ID card clipped to my belt. "What's your name?" I choke on the antiseptic smell, the slither of recycled air down my throat.

Ellis Karsten to the emergency department.

At first I think I'm hallucinating. Then the PA crackles again and repeats my name. *Ellis Karsten.*

They don't call people like me over the PA. I'm just another nurse at the triage desk, faceless, unmemorable. I've made it that way for our protection.

Unless it's Veer. Unless she needs me. No, there's nothing left there. That was clear enough when she hung up on me.

I mumble something about needing to get back to my floor, but the nurse has already turned her back on me, pushing the cart away, her mind moved on to other things. No one else stops me on the way out. I slip past the old woman, still waiting in her blue dress. I take the stairs all the way down, concrete echoing my footsteps into a wall of noise, and pause before the heavy door marked "G" for "Ground."

There are two ways out from here: through the sliding glass maw of the ED, or through the revolving doors of the south entrance, pushing against the stream of patients filing in for checkups and clinic visits.

South entrance will be emptied out, this time of night. ED's better.

I peek through the plexiglass window built into the door. I don't see anyone coming. When I shift to press my ear to the alien-smooth pane, I don't hear anything either. But the doors are heavy, and hunger's playing tug-of-war with my attention.

I wait for the PA to command me again, but it's fallen silent.

Back through the hallways. Don't flinch when someone passes. Don't let them know your veins are deserts.

I make it to the waiting room, and there's the door and the empty desk and Chaney standing in front of it, talking to a man with his hands on his belt and a stance that tells me he's with law enforcement before the khakis or the badge or the haircut even register. He stands looking down on her like his disdain is a gift, and Chaney smiles and twists a piece of hair that's escaped her bun because she's a good girl, she does what she's told, she wants to help.

And what am I?

It doesn't matter what I am, only that if this cop and his contempt lock me in a back seat with no handle, I will lose my mom and I will lose myself and I will become the thing I'm most afraid of. Chaney raises a hand like she's going to point, but not at me, she hasn't seen me yet.

Backtrack. South entrance.

The ceiling soars as the hallways open into the patient foyer, making space for plate-glass windows and two enormous indoor palms that flank the revolving doors. The floor is the same bile-yellow vinyl speckled with black flakes like bits of ash, but the chairs are nicer. A young man sits nearby, fidgeting with his phone. He keeps glancing at the bathroom door. I smell sweat-soaked shirt collars and the rancid floral desiccation of bacteria caught between flaps of aging skin. I wish I'd brought the pig's blood with me. Placebos are good for something, aren't they?

A flash of gold and my heart's in my throat. Another cop, same khakis, same posture, looming against the front desk. His scowl makes the monstera leaves on the receptionist's shirt look like they're wilting.

A woman waiting near the door tears at her cuticles. The cough drop scent of her denial and the blood dribbling from the cracks she's opening in herself, like too many painkillers and not enough sleep. My mouth floods with saliva, imagining the taste. If I'm detained, it'll prove one more time, the worst time, the truest time, that I'm the failure my mom's always accused me of being. If I'm detained, I'll lose her.

There has to be another exit.

There's not. I know there's not. What there *is* is another way out, one that means brutality in plain sight.

The cop at the desk is busy talking to the receptionist, and a gurney partially blocks me from view. I'm in scrubs. Just another nurse. Maybe all I have to do is stroll through the doors while his back is turned. Maybe, for once, I'll be lucky. Only after I take a step toward the door do I remember that hope is useless and I've never been lucky in my life.

My sneakers squeak on the vomit-colored vinyl and I smell the receptionist's aftershave, a hint at the movement that's coming before he's made it, and then he's pointing at me and the cop turns and they both see me.

"Excuse me," the cop calls. I skitter back toward the ED and another chance, but the hall fills with the slap of heavy boots as his partner closes in behind me. I'm afraid of them and for them, and for a second I'm outside myself, wondering how all of this happened, if any of it can be real.

"Excuse me, miss," he repeats, and it's all real and panic works its claws into the back of my neck. I can't remember how to breathe.

A nurse pushes through the space between us. Blood lingers in the hems of her scrubs. Hunger drives into my joints like screws twisting tight.

"You don't mind if we ask you a couple questions, do you?" It's the first cop, the one behind me. He smells like leather polish and plastic sunglasses warped in a hot car.

The beast in my chest growls. I need prey, I need carnage, I need somewhere to run. No, I need to get out. I need safety, and safety will never be around people. They're not like me. They're only meat.

"I can't," I choke out. Like they would understand. Like they care for explanations.

"Don't worry, it won't take you away from work for more than a few minutes." The second cop. He smells like sweat and Tootsie Rolls. He smells like a liar. I can feel his partner circling me.

My teeth jostle in the curve of my jaw. My wrists loose from their moorings. Their backs are so straight, necks thick under beige collars. They smell like certainty, like violence. They have holsters on their hips. Can I survive a gunshot? Can they survive me?

It's not a choice, it's an inevitability, to reach between my splintering ribs and throw the lock.

My kneecaps crack, my snout warps long and wicked. I smell the second cop's surprise as I lunge for him, sharp like a firecracker let off at close quarters, and then he's down and my jaws are wedged in his shoulder. My incisors scrape his collarbone. His artery is so close. I am single-minded and ravenous but his partner's drawn his gun and there's so much screaming.

"Step back!" I think he shouts, but I smell the twitch of his finger before the words leave him and spring away. My claws shred khaki shirtsleeve and the arm beneath and he's crawling too slow to catch me and blood is leaking from the other cop, more than there should be. Someone shot him. His partner fucking shot him.

My curse batters itself against my ruined rib cage and I careen forward. Hands in blood. Blood in mouth. It tastes like gas fumes and gunpowder. It tastes like heaven.

For a second, there's nothing but me and the blood that is paradise. Then I look up to see the woman who was tearing strips off her own cuticles with her eyes huge, scared pools of blue and her phone pressed to her ear.

Oh, right. I'm a monster.

Then the PA explodes with commands and I know I need to run.

23

I WRENCH MYSELF UPRIGHT. MY TEETH AND HANDS ARE human again by the time I slam through the revolving door. I sprint through the parking lot, away from the shouting and the blare of the PA, and if people turn to watch as I pass, I don't have time to look back. I'm gasping for breath when I reach my car. I twist the key so hard my finger bones shiver and I drive and drive and drive until the highway clears out and a sliver of space opens up in my thoughts.

Keep driving north, toward Corn Creek, toward the mountains. Toward the flayed man. This can't all be for nothing.

Blood on my hands has transferred to the steering wheel, and I wipe it off with the hem of my shirt. I try to burn the memory of the cop's limp form into my mind, try to make myself feel something. I should mourn for that man. I should mourn for Joanne. But I can't even mourn for myself. I'm an infection inside my own body, a bulbous growth displacing the natural order of my organs. All I can do is keep driving and promise myself that at the end, it'll mean something.

Mile markers flash by, white paint leering through their coatings of dust. Do I risk loosing my curse again to see if I can wrestle more direction from it before my hunger takes over? That mouthful of the cop's blood bought me a little more time, but only a little. I can't lose control. My head is so heavy. I haven't slept since when exactly? Yesterday morning? That seems hard to believe.

My mom and I once slept curled in the back seat of her car, driving through the heart of Oklahoma, the corn stretching flat and green as far as we could see. It shivered at night, the dry rustle of stalk against stalk like a lullaby as my mom twined her arms around me and promised that things would get better. She wore that sweatshirt, a gas station souvenir, and the pink glitter on the letters scraped the backs of my arms in my sleep.

"Soon, baby," I hear in her voice. "So soon. I promise. You trust me, don't you?"

But now she's gone, and I'm old enough to know that things never get better. Not for us.

Hunger digs its claws into my gums. I bite down, try to stifle it. Try, too, to stifle the grief that clings to me like a shadow, like a coat I can't take off.

I want to go home. But I can't, never again, not after what happened at the hospital. Someone almost certainly got a video of it, and if they didn't, there's always CCTV and the surviving cop's testimony. They've probably stormed our apartment by now and found the wreckage that the flayed man left when he took my mom.

I press my palm to the car window, let the night cold leach the sweat out of it. I hated leaving Colorado too. I fought it, as much as you can when you're fifteen and all twisted up inside. Some moms would have said something kind, about how home is with the people you love, not confined to our one-bedroom in Colorado Springs any more than the countless apartments and hotel rooms before it. That cheesy bullshit would have made me feel better, even if I couldn't admit it was what I wanted.

"Las Vegas was built in the middle of the desert," she'd said instead, elbow deep in dirty dishes. "The whole city, it's a mirage, baby. It's not supposed to exist, just like us. You'll see when we get there. A shiny city in the middle of the dustiest bowl of nothing, and it fights tooth and nail every day to stay that way. Just like us." She finished rinsing, set the mug down on the counter. "It'll be better, once we get there. My brother will take care of us."

Sixteen years is a long time to stay anywhere. Maybe what those years taught me is that home is a casino cashier desk where care is changed for obligation, but the exchange rate's steady and there's no threat of a robbery. Maybe that's as good as it gets.

My joints groan. I dig my knuckles into the scratchy fabric of the seat. If I don't feed soon, there's a serious chance that I'll find my mom only to lose control of my body. If I can't stay human, I'll burn in the daylight, no different from the flayed man. But there's nowhere else to steal from. I don't know the layout of any of the other hospitals, don't have access to Uncle Bill's work or another lab. The only option left is the oldest way, the hardest and worst way: violence.

What happened at the hospital shattered something in me, a glow stick deep in my skull that's cracked now, leaking poison fluid. I don't want to find out what killing would do to me.

But it's the smart choice. The safe choice. When someone's dead, they can't call the news or post on social media about the nightmare creature they saw with its bones on the wrong side of its skin. And I'll be alive. Isn't that what matters? If anything, the man I left behind at the hospital was worse, because I left him for dead and his blood with him. I can still taste it in the cracks of my lips. I suck on my fingernails, one by one, like there might be some still left in the crevices of my body. The desert smells like desperation. Or maybe that's me.

When I pull into a truck stop for a bathroom break, I think of the woman's terrified expression back at the hospital, and blink back tears. I miss my mom. She knows the worst parts of me, my ingratitude and selfishness, but she would never be horrified by this.

Her sweatshirt, hood pushed forward and sleeves pulled long over my balled fists, hides most of the blood still left on my shirt and skin. I wash my face in the sickly flickering light of the mirrorless bathroom and buy a radioactive-looking Slurpee to soothe my aching gums. The sugar leaves a coating like rotten fruit on my tongue. I move my car around the back of the truck stop, out of the way of the CCTV over the entrance. Then I perch on a pile of concrete blocks that form a half-hearted barrier between the asphalt and the desert and start counting security cameras.

It's the right choice. I repeat it until it tastes like a prayer. It's the right choice. And it is, I know it is, I just don't want to have to make it.

But I owe it to my mom to do whatever it takes. So I survey the highway as hunger sharpens my teeth. Waiting for someone alone or distracted or tired or high or drunk, someone who I can lure in close and catch off guard.

All the worst things I could imagine have already happened. What's one more?

24

WHEN I TURNED TWELVE, I STARTED GROWING LIKE A weed. At least, that's what my mom said. My knees ached in the night, and I suddenly needed twice as much food—and twice as much blood. A weed isn't a nice thing to have in your garden.

She was working at a convenience store, getting paid under the table, and they cut her hours out of nowhere, and when she got home, there I was, spitting feral teenage energy and eating everything in sight. Of course she lost her patience.

She stayed up all night tallying what she'd spent on me that year alone. Food, clothes, school supplies, gas. It was only April, but already my debt was unimaginable. She stuck it to the bathroom door so I'd see it every day, so I'd watch that number grow. I'd face it in the mornings and imagine what I'd owe by the time I turned eighteen. By the time I died. An unceasing mounting of cost, a quantitative measure of the thing I already knew could never be paid off. I tried to use the bathroom at school when I could, to avoid seeing it. I tried to eat less, to need less, to be less. I didn't like that school. The kids made fun of me for my clothes and for my silence.

When the bullying got real bad, they called my mom in for a meeting with some of the other parents. I sat in the hall outside, alone. All the other kids had after-school activities, sports or drama club or friends' houses to go to. So when my mom tore into those other parents like she was tempted to let go of the chain soldered to her heart, I was the only one who heard it.

"My daughter," she spat, and it must have been a shout because her words were fierce and clear while the others' responses were unintelligible, "is worth more than every other child in this school combined. I've sacrificed everything for her. Do you even know what sacrifice is? Do you really want to bring this fight to me? Do you really want to find out how hard I will come for you?"

Alone in the hall, I realized something. The same debt that loomed over me, that threatened to topple over and crush me, was also proof that my mom loved me. That she would give so much for me, that was something precious. That was a gift other children lived without and would never understand.

The next morning, there was no tally sheet on the bathroom door. We never talked about it again, but I remembered. Both things: the debt and its secret meaning.

I stay perched behind the truck stop, cinder blocks digging into my tailbone, and wait. Hunger rattles my soft palate. The 18-wheelers never seem to park outside the safety of the gas pumps and their CCTV.

Twenty minutes. Thirty. My phone's dying. Time's ticking.

Headlights cut through the early-morning emptiness. It's a truck, the same model as Uncle Bill's but silver instead of black. Maybe that's a sign. The driver's a younger guy, shaved head under a baseball cap and a T-shirt with angel wings on the shoulders. He's close enough to call out to. My throat feels like it's filled with gravel. Come on, say something. Get him over here. Say my engine's dead, that'll get him to move his car out of the way of the security cameras. And then—

All my joints shudder. My mind's suddenly plastered with an image of Veer, jacket stripped off to reveal her folded-in shoulders, bending over my car. Red in one hand, black in the other.

I can't force words through the rockslide in my throat, but I jerk my hand up in an impression of a wave. His attention twitches toward me at the same moment that my phone buzzes. A long, insistent purr, like it's got something special to tell me.

I glance down. It's a Reddit notification.

I forget the guy and snatch up my phone. Deep breath. Maybe they don't know anything. Maybe they've only written back to tell me to fuck off.

Hey, it reads. *I can't find the documentation anymore but I think it was a couple miles up Alamo Road or maybe Mormon Well, past the Corn Creek visitor center but before you fully get into the mountains. If you're not local, I can drive out and take some pics?*

Relief soaks through the rocks in my mouth. That's only a few miles away.

A second message blinks. *Are you okay? Why is it urgent?*

It's urgent because the sky is already threatening to fade from blue black to watery yellow. It's urgent because my veins are howling and I can either feed myself or find my mom before the sun comes up and the flayed man disappears into the crevices of the desert. There isn't time for both.

Unless.

The convenience store doors cough out the guy in the angel wings T-shirt, Monster energy can in hand.

"Hey," he calls, and for a second I don't realize he's speaking to me. He's got dark-brown eyes and a friendly smile, like no one's ever hurt him. "You good?"

I could do it right now. Bite down on his neck and make myself whole again. The sharp-toothed beast in my heart licks its lips. The bones of my face cry out for bloodshed.

Come on, Ellis. Do it.

His eyes aren't even the same color as hers. He's got thick, dark lashes, but the irises are muted and muddy and near black. Not the same, not brown like well-watered soil, like tea steeped so long it's perfectly bitter. His teeth are overly straight, the front four bright white and the rest ivory yellow. He smells like Irish Spring and eye drops. He's nothing like her.

And still. I can't.

A long second passes. The air smells like gas fumes and saliva. Every breath roils my stomach. All I can move is my eyes, and he must see something in them that looks like an answer because he shrugs and gets back in his car and drives away, and I only regain control over my limbs once they're crawling with the acidic sting of shame. My curse growls its contempt against my rib cage.

It doesn't matter. I don't matter. Every failure, every weakness, is meaningless, as long as I reach my mom in time. I'm strong enough to keep control of my hunger. I'll force myself to be strong enough.

I pull my car around and fill up the gas tank. Last thing we need is to run out of gas halfway to Arizona. The little screen on the gas pump flares to life, and a perky woman in a blazer blurts out a warning about hiking safety. *Don't forget to bring plenty of water!* The gas fumes make my eyes sting. They taste like olive pits and hopelessness. *Always tell a trusted friend or loved one where you're going!*

The nozzle clicks, and the screen fades to grainy news reruns. *Beloved Italian restaurant closing its doors after two decades. Golden Knights beat the Kings in their first preseason match.* Chaney's ex-boyfriend loved hockey. Preseason's in the fall, isn't it? How old are these headlines?

Doesn't matter. The pump spits out a flimsy receipt, and I ball it up and look for the trash. *Woman found dead in her apartment, shot by boyfriend. Search continues for San Diego man whose car was found off-road near Sheep Peak.*

My hand shudders, and the balled-up receipt bounces off the plastic lip of the trash can.

Sheep Peak. That's near Corn Creek, right? I double-check on the map. If you drove past the visitor's center and headed north, off-road, you'd end up somewhere near the base of Sheep Peak.

San Diego man. Off-road. This time, my search turns something up.

Raul Vargas, runner and IT guy in his thirties, up from San Diego on a road trip. Last seen at a gas station buying Red Bull and uncooked bacon. Cashier said he was acting erratic. They found his Subaru in the middle of the Desert National Wildlife Refuge, windows busted, a note written on the inside of the windshield in blood: *Gone hunting.*

Raul Vargas. RV.

Highway 95 is wide open. I shove the gas pedal down as far as it goes and try to ignore the pounding in my sinuses. The Joshua trees leer as I speed past.

I've known hunger all my life, but as the GPS counts down minutes and I lock stiff lips over my lengthening canines, I realize this is unknown territory. I've passed the point where I've always caught myself before, where I've always fed. I don't know what comes next, only that I have to keep myself from finding out before I reach my mom.

I don't need to ask my curse's help to scent the flayed man anymore. My hunger is so close to the surface our senses are melding. A vibrating ache spreads down my neck, seeps the length of my arms. A series of pops as my wrists begin to shift. The car veers toward the shoulder. Bite tongue, taste blood. My own, like ashes. Control it. Feeling springs back into my hands, and I jerk the wheel.

Gas pedal. Speedometer spikes. The horizon's the color of an orange cream popsicle. I remember the sugar taste of Veer's wounds. I weave around an oil tanker, jolt past a Prius.

Corn Creek, three miles away. Two. Next exit. My teeth jut over my lip, and for a second my vision goes white.

Control it. I'm so close.

Past the visitor's center. A sign says five miles per hour. There's a buzzing in my ears. Is my phone ringing, or is it only hunger snarling its demands through my eardrums?

It doesn't matter. It hurts to take my eyes off the cracks in the windshield and the faded brown expanse beyond it. I follow the flayed man's scent onto a dirt road, wheels throwing up a spray of dust and gravel. Keep going. My knees shudder, my ankles beg to come apart. Keeping my foot pressed down on the gas pedal is agony.

When the road craters into piles of rock and withered scrub, I park the car and jump out. The canyon walls look like opening jaws, and the impact of the ground under my feet almost brings me to my knees.

Something pops inside me. Broken rib. It hurts, it must hurt, but it's hard to tell when all my bones are screaming. I shove my arm between my teeth and bite down. Skin breaks. My curse howls.

Maybe I can catch a rabbit. A snake. Anything I can drain of its blood, anything to keep me contained. But this is the desert, there's nothing here I can outsmart or outrun, and if I let go, I will turn inside out and lose myself and not know how to get back.

I take a step. My ankle rolls on gravel. I try to remember my name. My mom. Focus on that. He took my mom. The smell is so strong now. He's nearby. They both are.

I double over as another rib snaps. My phone buzzes in my pocket. I can't reach for it. My wrists shatter in slow motion, lacerations snaking up my arms, daring my elbows to join them. Cartilage warps in anticipation. I've made a mistake. I've made such a mistake. Soon the animal in me will punch through my chest, and I will not be able to save my mom, and I will not be able to save myself.

High above, a hawk shrieks. I smell motor oil and dust-slick metal on the wind. A plume of dust from the direction of the road, heading this way. A way out.

I'll flag them down. I'll bury my jaws in the driver's throat.

My cracked ribs shriek as I lift my arms above my head. Blood from my lacerated ankles pools in my sneakers. My elbows shift and snap, and wetness—sweat? blood? synovial fluid?—whirls around me like snowflakes as I wave.

The parched ground laps up my collapsing body, and the car rumbles to a stop.

A dented silver Camry.

"Ellis?" She smells like singed cotton and the sugar stickiness of a spilled energy drink. "I'm sorry if you don't want to see me, but I heard something happened at work and you weren't picking up my calls and I checked the location and you were out here and I just wanted to make sure you were okay and . . ."

I'm going to be sick. I grasp for the chain, but my fingers have curled into claws and there's no purchase on the iron.

The car door slams. My throat closes. The blood coursing under her skin smells like eggs from the late-night diner, like burnt rubber and desperation. It smells like home.

I'm so, so hungry.

"Don't—" I try to say, but the words catch on my warped incisors. I struggle again for purchase. Pull back. Ten seconds, even, just enough to get her back in the car with a plate of metal between us. Pull, Ellis. Pull. But my name has no meaning when I'm only instinct.

Veer freezes in place, halfway between me and the car. In a half second of lucidity, I see the terror on her face. I don't look like myself. I'm cracking open. I lunge forward, double over, and she jerks away.

Another rib pops. My sternum sighs and splinters. The beast in my rib cage barrels toward freedom.

Veer backs up. "Oh my god," I think she says. Words don't mean much anymore. I'm on all fours, shoulders sliding like tectonic plates to spread open my chest. The air goes charred as Veer's engine turns over.

The flayed man's scent overwhelms me. Quartz fragments

and creosote and days-old carrion. The stink of decay, of the desert's harsh corrosion, of rotten flesh and empty canyons, the sharp snap of a hawk's claws.

Then yellow light.

It feels like it's coming from inside me, bubbling up from the base of my throat, exploding out of my eyes to blind me. The brown-gray-blue of the world is replaced with a flat screen of dazzling yellow. My curse lunges forward, whining as if its legs are being piloted against its will.

Dust in the air. Veer driving away. I blink again, and the road is filled with blood.

The Camry's wheels churn uselessly, and without warning it swerves to the left, off-road, and stops with an ear-splitting crunch.

I want to scream. It comes out a howl. I see a canyon before a flash flood, rocks cast pyre red with excitement, chalk white with anticipation.

The flayed man paints one final message across my mind as I turn to face him.

Give up.

25

MY FIRST IMPULSE IS TO LET GO OF THE CHAIN, LET brutality infect me, let my jaws grow so long they'll run him through. I'll burn when the sun comes up, same as he will, but that happens slow and violence can happen fast.

But I need him alive. He knows where my mom is. And through the queasy stench of decay, I can still smell Veer. If I let go completely, what happens to her?

Don't bother.

Asphalt shimmering on an August highway. Creosote crackling underfoot.

It won't work.

Fuck you. I reach for the waiting chain, and—oh. He's right. My curse is paralyzed, suspended midleap, ears pressed flat to its skull and eyes roving desperately. My knees are still bent back, my elbows still weeping, but it's not getting any worse.

My body is my own to destroy. Who is he, to be allowed such power over it?

"Where's my mom?" I demand.

The strands of muscle around his mouth draw back in a ghoulish smile. I look up into his lidless eyes and his deathless, worm-woven face, and my senses are caked with the smell of rot.

"You want to see her." It's not a question, and it's no longer in my mind but spoken out loud in a voice that sounds like it hasn't been used in centuries. The chasm in his torso pulses.

"Please." It rips out of me, almost like I'm not speaking at all. Please. I came all this way, I fought my body for every step, and not even because I owe her. Though I do, I do, that's been carved into the lining of my organs and I can't escape it. It's because I need her, because she's my home and she's all I have left, and because if she's stolen from me now, then what was the point of fighting my whole life to be enough for her? What's it all been for, if she can't look at me and finally say she's satisfied?

The flayed man's torso spasms, and he laughs a raw, scraping noise that sounds like torture. From somewhere behind me comes an answering howl. Loping animal footfalls. The smell of rancid yogurt and pink lipstick, silk pillowcases and rose hand cream, but scorched and sticky, caramelized by viciousness. Before, I would have sworn I'd die before I ever saw my mom turned monstrous. But now . . .

"Mom?" My voice cracks. I know it's her. I'd know her anywhere, even like this. Skinless and bestial, head hung low between exposed shoulder blades, her chest a writhing mass of maggots. She folds herself at the flayed man's feet and vomits a sound halfway between a sob and a snarl. Her dull gray eyes weep a milky mixture of blood and vitreous fluid.

Worms ripple over the mountain ranges of the flayed man's sharklike fangs. "You're welcome."

"What did you do to her?"

"She chose the hunt." I'm flooded with more images. A desert-bleached neon sign, glass jagged, corrupted by sand. A leg, fleshy, then gangrenous, then stripped to bone, while clouds speed overhead.

"What about my uncle?"

The flayed man coughs, a sound like canyon walls scraping together. He coughs again, and this one sounds like a botched operation. I can see the heave of his throat echoed in the empty space of his chest, and then I'm not looking at him at all because I smell blood. Like instant coffee and engine oil and veins so pickled by chemicals and resentment that they've forgotten there's any other way to be. Then I see what he's vomited up.

The desert constricts until the only things in the world are my useless body and the flayed man's worm-ridden tendons and the half-digested heart that he's puked onto the sand in front of me. It weeps blood into the cracks of the desert. Worms untwist themselves from the flayed man's wrecked tendons and drop onto it, fat pale teardrops burrowing into withered muscle.

"He came to visit too. But he wasn't ready to hunt."

Behind him, my mom climbs to her feet. In this form, her bones are no longer brittle, her body no longer frail. She rolls her shoulders, and skinless muscle ripples.

"Mom," I beg. "It's me. It's Ellis. Don't you want to go home?"

She paces a slow half circle around the flayed man. Her milky eyes lock not on my face but on my throat. "Please, Mom. You know me. You remember me."

The flayed man paws the dirt. His skinned feet are split

in the center, more hoof than human and crowned by the wreckage of shattered ankle joints. "And you? What will you choose?"

The abyss of his mouth ripples. The snarl that emerges burrows into me like cactus spines, and I hear the command in it: *Attack*.

But he's frozen my curse. I can't lose control. Not because I'm stronger, but because he won't let me. I don't understand, and then a body hits me and I'm down, razor teeth snapping the shadows at the back of my neck, and I do.

The command wasn't for me.

"Mom!" I get my legs under me just in time to dodge her flashing teeth, coming for my neck again. She lunges and I rear back, arms up to protect my face, and I'm on my back, claws slicing through layers of muscle and tendon where I try to push her away.

"It's me." I'm trapped between two forms, only half metamorphosed, but she's all animal. "Please—"

Her snout twists and my forearm goes white-hot. Blood froths over her teeth. I wrench my arm free and kick myself upright, praying she missed the artery. When we face off again, my mom crouches low on her haunches, a predator's growl leaking between her teeth.

She's not in there anymore. She's going to kill me.

I think of the knife in my bag and Uncle Bill's conviction and all the reasons I swore I couldn't, I wouldn't, it wasn't time yet. And when she leaps for me again, I know I have to.

I sidestep and launch myself at her. She skids on the hard-packed ground, writhing under my weight. Her heart pulses frantically, dirt-spattered and exposed. My teeth are long and sharp enough, even half-transformed like this.

My snout is poised at the cavity of her rib cage when she whines. Tragic, desperate. I look into her face and see those eyes, her eyes, gray, unfocused, weeping. Is this how I show her I love her?

I turn my face away from hers, back to the heart I'm meant to skewer. The flayed man took my compassion and made it cruel. Made it some vengeful game.

I can't do it. Not even if it kills me.

The flayed man growls. "Pathetic."

Then he's knocking me out of the way, aiming for her heart, and I realize what he's doing a split second before he does it and I won't let him. She's my family and he's nothing, and he won't take this away from me. I coil all my strength into my legs and barrel into him. The flayed man rolls free of my mom, and before I can think what it will do to me, I wrench my fist through the wreckage of her rib cage and impale all four red-purple ventricles with my claws.

I pull free and sink into the dirt. My face is wet. Someone is screaming. I only realize it's me when my throat gives out.

I brace for the burn of the flayed man's fangs. But he doesn't attack. He sniffs my mom's corpse, dives his snout into the reliquary of her chest. I squeeze my eyes shut.

Footfalls, and his scent draws closer. When I open my eyes, his circular void of a mouth is level with them. Fresh hot blood coats his jagged teeth.

Her heart is in his mouth.

He grins wide and snaps his jaws shut. My mom's blood spatters my face, warm and wet. The flayed man's esophagus bulges as he swallows.

"You're pitiful." A vast, impersonal *you* that means all of us, anyone like me. He pronounces it like it's the worst thing he can imagine. "Self-absorbed, petty. Fearful. Killing's supposed to be fun, isn't it?"

I won't answer. I can't answer. My throat is slick with tears.

"Isn't it?" he snarls. His mouth flares, and endless rows of blackened teeth rise to meet me, writhing with fat worms and remnants of my mother's heart.

Something's rising in me too. Something primal. Something angry.

Petty, boring, pathetic, selfish. I've heard all that before, and no cruel words or rotted worms can scar me or scare me more than my mom can. And she's gone now. He took her from me and chewed her heart up like it was nothing. I want to rip him apart, piece by piece. I want to show him what it's like to be eaten alive by guilt and shame. I want failure to kiss him on the mouth and make him bleed.

"I can see the future," he hisses. "I'm going to eat your heart, and then I'm going to eat your friend too."

For a second, I'm derailed, but then I realize it's all a con, a threat, a maneuver. These are the kinds of games humans play. Name-calling, negging, lies. Here is a creature who thrives on the hunt, on the slip of heart muscle through his teeth, here is a legend passed on through generations, who can stalk into my mind, who can conjure corrosion before my eyes, and he's playing games. My anger soars higher and higher, searing white-hot with injustice. But like a fire, there's only so much for it to eat, and when it falters, fear rushes in. Would it be so bad to die? the fear whispers. If I just close my eyes, soon none of this will be real.

If only I wasn't so alone.

And then a howl.

Not an animal one, a human one, rage and vengeance. She comes out of nowhere, something thick and silver in one hand, and without a hitch in her step she swings it over her head. The tire iron misses the flayed man's skull but cracks onto his shoulder, and he goes down with a screech and a spray of blood.

"Eat that, motherfucker!" Veer shouts. Her eyes are huge, her voice is too loud. Terror, shock, probably both. She tries to offer me a hand. God, I want to take it. But what happens when the flayed man's paralysis lifts? Where does that leave me and the hunger ready to crawl out of my skin?

"Get out of here." I hate the way my voice sounds, raspy and muddled. "I can't—"

The flayed man rises from where she crumpled him. Veer's scream smears red across my vision.

I was angry before. Now, I'm not anything. I'm just an animal.

26

MY CHEST EXPLODES IN WET AGONY, AND THEN I'M different, pelvis twisting, knees cracking backward, fangs shearing through the soft flesh of my lower lip as I fight to not bite off my own tongue. Instinct blurs my thoughts to pinpricks of sensation.

I cling to my sanity and point my fury toward the flayed man.

I hit him like a car accident. My claws snap through his rotting tendons like guitar strings as I tear him off Veer. She lands limp on her back.

The flayed man laughs hoarse and harsh, like the whir of a garbage disposal. His blood-soaked arms snake out, and I hit the ground with enough whiplash to blur my vision. His hoof-foot digs into the cavernous remains of my torso, and reality goes blurry at the edges.

"This isn't going to change anything," he snarls. "Stop trying."

I spit blood and saliva and wrath up at him. It froths over my lips but goes no farther. He shifts his weight, and my head spins with the sound of a thousand bowls shattering as the edges of my ruined rib cage slice black ribbons across the skinned soles of his feet. Thick, heavy drops weep into the void of my chest, and I feel a twisting in my lungs, like his worms have slithered their way inside.

He steps back and I roll myself over, try to get back on all fours. My claws slip on the hard-packed ground. The flayed man laughs again.

"Have you ever eaten a heart?" he asks. Something's broken in my pelvis. No, everything's broken. My lips won't close over my teeth. Instinct pilots my legs under me, and I try to hold on to a sliver of myself by reciting the names of bones. Ilium. Sacrum. Coccyx.

"Of course not." He's on all fours too now, thrusting his snout in close. Frontal bone. Nasal bone. Maxilla. Mandible. "You wouldn't dare. But I've lived a thousand years and I've dared a thousand times, and for you I'll make it a thousand and one."

He leans over me, and worms emerge from his flesh like white threads. They land on me like raindrops, wriggling where they touch exposed skin. On my arm, one lifts a delicate head to expose a faceless abyss of teeth.

Scapula. Humerus. Radius. Ulna.

Those tiny teeth kiss me, and with the latch of its mouth my senses light up with countless other tiny pressure points, other worms. The flayed man crouches low, one taloned foot tracing the rupture in the center of my chest. I imagine my heart there on display, no longer protected by ribs or flesh or iron.

Cervical. Thoracic. Lumbar.

The worms carve cavities into my musculature. The flayed man's touch shaves away the iron woven through my skeleton.

I'm losing control and I can't get away and I'm buckling, weakening.

Femur. Tibia. Fibula. Patella.

The flayed man's hand catches behind the barbed wire of my broken ribs and I forget every name of every bone I ever learned in nursing school.

I'm going to die, and it's my fault.

No. Not like this. I won't be a sacrifice to something who only sees me as the next in a line of a thousand faceless sacrifices. I'm a monster and a ruin and a daughter without a mother and I'm going to kill him right fucking back.

I let go of the final shreds of control and my curse rears up with a scream so loud it burns my tongue. His fingers scrape my lungs and then my claws are tearing through him, snapping bone as the worms infecting me squirm impotently. Claws aren't enough. I dive my snout into the ruin of his chest cavity and my dagger fangs close around the pulsing sac of blood and flesh and power inside. I rip free, and the animal I am howls something ancient and unholy through my mouth as I bite down. My mouth floods with a taste like stale breath and ancient magic.

Eventually, he stops fighting.

I blink, and all that's left of him is a wet stain brushstroked across the dirt. I watch it seep into the indifferent throat of the desert. My stomach clenches, and I retch up a mouthful of white worms. All dead. I dip my snout and wrench the rest of them out of me by their tails. They burst under my claws, and the desert rushes to absorb their innards.

Brightness is starting to crest the mountains, but the sun isn't up yet. My curse is me and I am my curse, and I haven't lost control. I'm alive, I'm pure animal, I'm realer than I've ever been. The air is iridescent with scent. Scarred metal and day-baked dirt, sick blood like iron filings and choked-up organs, and healthy blood like panic and pain. And fear. Fear that clogs my nose and seeps into my brain, fogging my thoughts.

It's coming from behind me.

Hunger scrapes my shins. I turn and there's Veer, huddled against her busted-up car. The one surviving headlight illuminates her from below like a ghoul. Rusty spatters paint her shirt, a red welt works its way across her neck. Her eyes are dark as the mountains at night, and huge with terror.

She smells good. She'd taste so much better.

My lips curl back into a snarl. Veer twitches and tries to get her legs underneath her but can't quite get her balance. Power coils in my hips.

"Ellis?" she rasps, and I remember the way she laughed as we flew through the desert, the way she brandished that tire iron like an apocalypse, and the way she's already started to keep my secrets. I could tear her throat out and bury the only person who could betray me. And where would that leave me? Alone. Is that what I want?

I don't want to be like the flayed man, skinless and desert born and scheming. I don't want to be like my mom, grasping for love and ending up only pitied or owed. I want to sweep Veer into my arms, to fall to my knees, to explain everything. I want to try.

I can have that, still. I can fold myself back into human form before the sun is bright enough to burn me. I can fix this.

"Don't be scared," I try to say, but it comes out a clatter of jaws and saliva.

I try to step back. Nausea hits me like the aftermath of bones breaking. The animal rushes in, forcing my feet back to the ground, and suddenly we're in a tug-of-war in the muscles of my legs and I'm dizzy and it's so strong, stronger than it's ever been and it'll do anything to stay free from its cage.

I try again. Step back. My curse rears, defiant, and my vision blurs and I careen forward. Veer flinches back into the wrecked car's embrace, mouth half-open, breathing fast.

"Okay," she repeats, more to herself than me. "Okay, okay, okay . . ."

She smells like polyester and panic and the raw scrape of a split lip. One more leap, and I won't be hungry anymore.

Desperation pushes and I pull, and we reel drunkenly onto all fours and there's a slam and a scramble and Veer's inside the car now. Relief. Rage. My animal turns dinner-plate eyes on me, as if I've betrayed it.

She's going to drive away. That's what she was supposed to do in the beginning.

The passenger door flies open. She comes back. My hunger-addled limbs are too surprised to lunge. I am too, until I see the camping knife in her hand. Green handle, silver blade. Veer's face is blank now, the grim mask of detachment she wears at work.

So that's what it's come to.

My mind smears with something like *This is what it always comes to* and I'm not going to die, I'm not, my mouth is full of blades and I'll do whatever it takes, but that doesn't stop me from feeling like someone's plunged their claws into the weeping wound of my chest and separated the pieces of my heart.

Veer blows out a sharp breath and cradles the knife in the crook of her elbow.

"Hey," she mumbles. "This'll help, right?"

I don't understand, until she breathes out sharp and fast and her arm bends, and I smell blood like distrust and devotion. Still, I half expect her to attack me. She offers me her arm, and I smell her fierce, well-guarded tenderness, and still I half expect.

Go slow, I beg, but I'm pistoned forward and my snout is on her skin and Veer yelps a little as her blood wells into my mouth. I close my eyes and taste bruised fruit and the golden of sunset, and the creature in my bones recedes until it's just me and the faint whispering clank of metal and my furious certainty that both of us have to survive this, because what else has it all been for? I reach back inside myself, and my palms brush twisted iron. There's no cage left anymore. No chain.

What if I was everything my curse made me? What if I could be hungry, dangerous, a portent of evil, and all the other things my family made me, what if I could be all that and still, too, be myself?

I squeeze her arm gently between my teeth, wanting more. The desert is broad and harsh and filled with wonders, and so is the world. And so am I.

A soft growl. I reach for it, find fur and longing. Touch the places where its claws left long hungry grooves in my rib cage. The growl trails into a whine, long and thin and plaintive, and I realize that it's tired too. A lifetime of denial and iron, of a chain fused to its spine and the promise of agony at the end of freedom, made it something that leapt and fought and dragged its tired, shivering body back to the loneliness of captivity.

Maybe now we can try something different.

Pain grabs hold of my larynx. My marrow goes wobbly,

my joints grind back into position, my knees unbreak and my fangs recede and my ribs creep back into the crimson hollow of my chest. I'm still bent over Veer's arm, kissing the fragrant pink-red line she's made for me. She shifts and I try to follow but I'm gelatinous inside, pain splintering up my shins and vibrating through my spine, and suddenly I'm doubled over and vomiting a mix of acidic foam and decomposing worms into the dirt.

My hands are too small. I touch my face with my fingers. Nose cheeks lips chin. Blood everywhere, sticking my shirt to my neck, soaking my hair dark and stringy.

Don't look at Veer. She's seen too much, she'll never stop seeing it. Of course I look at her. She's a wreck and she's radiant and she's the only real thing in the world. I want to wrap my arms around her and bury my face in the soft skin behind her ears. I want to tell her I'll never hurt her, unless she wants me to, unless she'll hurt me back. I want, I want, I want.

Her eyes flutter. She coughs, dry and embarrassed, and snaps the knife shut, and I remember that I'm lying in a pool of my own vomit.

"Well, shit," she says. "You scared me for a second."

I hack up a laugh. It feels good. She helps me to my feet and her fingers linger, just for a moment, to trace the wreckage of my chest. The wound's still weeping through my shirt. It'll close soon. My bones are already fusing back to rightness.

We limp back to her car, her hand stroking my blood-soaked hair, my fingers counting her ribs through her shirt, and every part of the world turns to dust except where her skin meets mine.

27

VEER'S CAR DOESN'T START. MINE'S SOMEWHERE UP THE road. Both of our phones are ruined, so there's no calling a mechanic.

We perch together in the back seat of her Camry and split a pack of wet wipes. The damp squares smell like antiseptic and sting like it too, cutting slashes through the dirt and sweat and fluids we're both caked in. We stack the used wipes on the center console like offerings on an altar. I manage to wipe away the worst of the gore, but there's still dried blood tugging at the edge of my scalp, slicking under my nails and all the other hard-to-scrub places.

I don't want to talk about my mom. Veer seems to know and doesn't ask.

The memory of her fangs still snaps at the back of my neck. Her clouded eyes, her undimmed viciousness. I was so caught up in my last duty, my promise of absolution. I was so certain I needed to earn her forgiveness. What if, instead, I was the one who needed to forgive her?

What if I still can? What if, too, I can still forgive myself?

We hike back in the growing glow of morning until we find my car. The sun catches on the spiderweb cracks in the windshield. The ghost of the last true thing I said to my mom—*This is why I hate you* and *I'll never be good enough for you* and *You need me more than I need you*—pricks my mouth. No, wait. That wasn't it. I remember the slip of her hair under my fingers, the softness of her silk pillowcase. Her murmur of *The desert was so beautiful that day.*

It was, Mom. It was.

I look up at where the mountains grin with centuries-honed teeth, opening their arms to the dawn. It still is.

Veer drives with the windows rolled down. The wind whips my face so furiously I close my eyes. My wounds knit themselves closed in the passenger seat, my chest creaking each time my lungs expand. The wind shifts to kiss the back of my neck as we turn into the driveway of an off-white bungalow, past a thicket of long-withered rosebushes, and roll to a stop in front of Veer's garage apartment.

"Come in," she says. "I'll order pizza."

Her place isn't much, a mattress on milk crates, folding chairs around a plastic table. Someone—lots of someones—have drawn all over the table in black and red. Hearts and stars and *so-and-so was here*. A squiggle of a gun with a red flag sticking out of the barrel reading, *BANG!* Mickey Mouse with drooping red eyes and bloodstained teeth. I look at it, at all the signs of adventure and vitality and an attempt at life, at being someone who doesn't ever hide, and I'm gripped by a sudden feeling of lack.

Veer kicks a cardboard box, and it skids into a corner. "It's not much. Sorry."

"It's nice." My voice cracks like I haven't spoken in years.

"When my, uh. I know it's not the same thing. But it helps to talk sometimes. Even just to say the dark stuff out loud. And I mean, even if you don't want to, if there's anything else . . ."

I think of the maroon paint in the motel, and the relief of saying all the things I was afraid would make me treacherous. Something hums, just for a second, in the dark wetness of my chest cavity. Then it's gone, and I'm back to pretending that I don't feel scooped out and replaced, and that I'm not terrified that I'm worse now, somehow.

"Not right now."

In the shower, I watch the water fade from murky reddish to clear and feel like I'm losing something. When I emerge, Veer has unpacked the car. My mom's suitcase is lying there next to my bag, and I can't look at it without wanting to sob. It's all real. It's real, and I have to live with it, and worst of all, I have to make sense of it.

When the pizza comes, I find I can't put it into my mouth without gagging. Instead, I eat saltines from the back of the cupboard. Veer leaves to get a rental car, pick up some groceries and extra towels and new phones, those pay-as-you-go ones that are cheap from the supermarket, and I unzip my duffel bag and find the knife that was meant for my mom and then I'm sobbing again, and that's what the saltines were for, to replace all the salt I'm crying out, enough for an ocean, enough to drown in.

I keep waiting for Veer to come back and find me like this, stretched out pathetic on her floor, but she doesn't. Then out of nowhere I'm not crying anymore. Because I don't have any tears left, maybe, but something else too. Maybe this is what Veer tried to tell me. That if I had a choice, it wouldn't have happened how it did, but now that it's done, there's more space for me as I am. Not the daughter my mom wanted. Not the caretaker I twisted myself into.

My animal presses its nose to my ribs, and its liquid eyes say, You're right. The future is a highway through the desert, and I can take it anywhere I want to go.

I boot up my laptop. My inbox is choked with bill-pay alerts, marketing newsletters. And a new thread from an email group called *map-western-us.* The name is a little familiar, but I don't remember subscribing to it. Then I open it, and I do.

Interesting visitor this morning, reads the first one, from sender Brian NV. *Bill K's grown-up niece. If you have anything to say to her, she's here.*

Uncle Bill had an email from this group, one that didn't load. It was such an innocuous name, and such an old message, that I didn't even wonder what it was. This must be why Brian wanted my email address.

There are replies too. One from Anita Santa Fe: *Welcome, if you're ever in New Mexico, please reach out. We live on a beautiful ranch with horses. There is a hospice just down the road.* Another from Carlos SLC: *did bill say it was ok to add her bro thats effed up if not.* Over that, from Bill T Boise: *You hit reply all again man.*

I stare at the phone as the messages blink from "unread" to "read," one by one. All those veiled hints about living life, about leaving my mom—why didn't Uncle Bill tell me he was in touch with all these others like us? Sixteen years, two-thirds of them adult ones, and he never once thought to? Never thought I'd want to know? Was he scared we'd find someone else to supply our blood, and leave him?

That doesn't sound like Uncle Bill, though. That sounds like my mom.

I remember Brian's cleared throat, the awkwardness after he said he'd found Uncle Bill through the map. That's what this is, must be. *Right. Your mom is Bill's crazy sister.* And I decide that I don't want to know.

My mom is gone. It doesn't matter.

When Veer gets back, she fiddles with her phone for a second—it's so new it's still missing a case—then thrusts the screen toward me.

"You're in the *Review-Journal*," she says.

Police Officers Involved in Shooting at Sunrise Hospital, the headline reads. I snatch it from her hands and start scrolling.

The woman attempted to attack the officers and run, according to the Metropolitan Police Department, the story reads. *One of the officers drew a gun during the chase. Officer Bucklee has been employed with the department since 2015.*

The worst night of my life, flattened into a few quotes at a press conference. The story doesn't include my name. No mention, either, of my transformation. It's easier to deny things when they seem impossible.

"Ying said they got him straight to the OR," Veer murmurs. "If he was dead, the headline would be different."

She holds out her hands, and I drop the phone back into them.

"Tell me the real story?" she asks quietly, like she's afraid she'll spook me. I swallow and taste dust and blight and the salt of my own tears, and suddenly, the words are there.

"My family's cursed." I scratch at my arm without thinking, and my nails reopen one of the many cuts the flayed man speckled me with. My blood still smells like him. "Well, that's the easiest way to describe it, at least. Not in a special way. In a sick way. I mean, my body's just like yours, mostly, except for there's something extra inside."

Veer's face doesn't change, exactly, just tightens, and I remember that she's seen it—the gaping wound of my chest, the alien inversion of my joints, the scimitar canines curving over my warped jawbones.

"Blood keeps the curse buried. Three, four milliliters a day. My uncle used to steal it from UNLV, he worked in a lab there. But he's gone, same as my mom. When we drove out together to see your brother, I was getting some more from this guy who has a lab in his basement." I swallow, remembering the dead beep of Brian's disconnected phone. "But that was a one-time thing."

Veer nods slowly, and I smell apprehension on her breath. "And now?"

I'm no good at stealing. I'm worse at killing. I don't want to be resentful like Uncle Bill, or a parasite like my mom. I wish I knew what else there was to be.

"I don't know." Every word weighs me down. "There's no killing it. Not without killing the rest of me too."

Veer's been looking at the floor, playing with her cuticles, but now her eyes rise to meet mine and I'm blinded again by the high-beam intensity of her stare. "Why would you want to kill it?"

For a fresh start. A life without the specter of family or flayed men, where I owe nothing and have no secrets. Would she understand that?

Veer absentmindedly rubs at the still-fresh cut on her arm, and the air fills with a smell like jasmine blossoms and sharpened stakes. "Three or four milliliters, huh. That's not so bad. A person could lose that much blood every day, no problem."

She looks at the floor again, and then up at me through her lashes, and sort of half smiles. Her eyes are dark and desperately generous, and suddenly I understand what she's offering.

I can't take it. Can I?

A fresh start. Can't fuckin' die in Nevada.

Veer saw me in all my grotesque animal fury and still came after me. Maybe she'll learn to resent me, or I'll learn to hate her, but isn't that what I wanted? I mean, the chance to try something new and the freedom to turn away from it when I want, on my terms. And I won't have to lie or steal or carve pieces of myself off as offerings to the gods of loneliness to survive. At least for a little while.

I want to say *Why?* and *What's wrong with you?* and maybe, just a little, *What's wrong with me?* There's a roughness in my throat, and it takes a second to realize I'm on the verge of tears. Because I'm scared, fuck, I'm scared that the future might be good, and it feels like betraying my mom to look forward to it.

"That could get old quick," I say, and Veer shrugs and I'm gripped with the urge to say more, to say everything, to get on my knees and swear to her that I'll never hurt her, that my curse will never touch her, but that's not true and I think she'd know I was lying.

I shuffle forward and reach across the gap between us until I can tap the back of her hand with one finger. "Can we go for a drive?"

So we drive. Veer winds through the neighborhoods, going

nowhere in particular. Just going. Maybe she'll drive in circles till the sun goes down, till time stops. Her knuckles are striped pink and white against the black foam of the steering wheel.

"Are you going to tell anyone?" I whisper.

Without warning, Veer pulls over. She shoves her hand into her pocket and then there's her open palm and the snick of a blade, and before I can react, her hand is on my mouth and my sinuses are full of the scent of calamity and collapse. I lick the line she's opened, a sort of second heart line, and my body crackles with the electric energy of sacrifice and satiation. No more blood that smells of preservation and penitence. She tastes like coming home.

"What do you think?" she says, her eyes on the horizon, her sweat on my lips.

I press my tongue flat against the cut, willing it to close, and pull away.

"Your palm's a stupid place to cut. It'll keep reopening."

Veer retracts her hand, her eyes dark. "I'm counting on it."

I want to kiss her. I want so many things, but there's a dusty, dented pickup truck a few houses down with a red-and-black *For Sale* placard in the window and that feels like a sign.

I nod at the truck. "I'm going to go take a look at it."

Veer tenses. The air goes stale, and I'm flooded with the familiar feeling of failure. I've ruined everything again, somehow.

"Okay," she mutters as I climb out. I want her to stop me. I want her to put into words what she wants from me and what she wants to give me. I don't know how to do this.

Veer looks miserable, and I'm struck by the thought that maybe she doesn't either. I remember the way she lashed out, the cold snap of her *Can I help you?* She watched me so many times, she waited for the right moment, and when it came, she couldn't stop herself from pushing me away.

What if I tried, one more time, to get it right?

I slip back into the passenger seat. Veer's hand flinches back from the gear shifter, her eyes flashing amber with hope.

"Hey," I say. Wrong. Bad start. Stupid. Get out of the car, Ellis. Run away. Disappear. I breathe through my nose, let myself get lost in the cocoon of brake dust and sticky candy wrappers and a heart-line cut still refusing to close.

"I used to wish for someone like you," I tell the blue expanse outside the windshield, and my voice wavers. "Someone who'd see everything, and not be scared, or maybe even be scared, but not turn away. Someone who'd take care of me without making it a debt."

In the driver's seat, Veer makes a choked noise. I turn and her eyes are glittering. She folds her hand over mine, envelops me in the smell of possibility and promise.

"I think I wished for someone like you too," she whispers. She sniffs, hides it with a cough. "You don't owe me shit, okay? When you were"—her hands flit uncertainly between her mouth and her torso, and I realize she's still finding words for what I am—"that was the scariest thing I've ever seen, no question, but I've seen a lot of scary shit. I can take it. Just, you know, I want someone who'll take from me honestly. Not fuck me up and call it love."

She trails off, and I hear all her secrets in the silence after. She, too, is afraid of being in debt. She, too, doesn't know how to love without sacrificing pieces of herself. But life is long and the desert is wide and maybe there's still time to try.

I look back to the sign on the truck. *89K miles. Good condition.* The desert and its endless hunger, that's home—the long straight stretch of highway, the mirage glimmer as it cuts a fork in the lapping tongue of the mountains. Maybe some of these strangers in my inbox are too much like my mom, or like Brian, but maybe some of them aren't.

"I have to go," I say, and her fingers grip hard into mine. "But trucks have passenger seats."

Her hand's on my chin, now, forcing me to look at her. "Don't fuck with me, now."

She looks dangerous. Relief grows, expands out of me. "I won't."

She pushes into me, lips scraping mine, but the kiss itself is gentle and tender and scared and hopeful. Maybe there is something warmer than loneliness. Easier than fear. Maybe I can have it. Maybe I can't, but fuck it, it's at least worth a try.

Veer settles back in the driver's seat, and I dial the number.

ACKNOWLEDGMENTS

Thank you to my agents, Amanda Orozco and Laura Cameron. I'm so grateful for your advocacy, advice, and tireless support for this book and for myself as an author.

Thank you to Dan López and Dan Smetanka, who not only saw my vision but put into words pieces of the story that I didn't yet have words for. Your insight and ideas have made *The Flayed Man* better in innumerable ways.

Thank you to cover designer Victoria Maxfield, production editor Laura Berry, copy editor Marie Landau, the marketing/PR team, including Megan Fishmann, Rachel Fershleiser, and Andrea Córdova, events manager Lily Philpott, and the many others at Soft Skull who made this book a reality.

Thank you to everyone who read and critiqued early versions, especially Soon Jones and M. R. Edgeworth, who helped me get the end in order. Thank you also to Alex Brown and Justine Pucella Winans for always cheering me on and teaching me everything I know about plot.

Thank you to my family for your ceaseless support and enthusiasm. How lucky I am to have a family I not only love, but also really like.

My love—thank you for believing in me before the beginning. And AK—I love you!!!

© Phrachan Thewi

CHLOE LAUTER is an entertainment publicist in Los Angeles.